# Stranded

**Fiction**

Alexis Jones

Published by Alexis Jones, 2024.

STRANDED

**First edition. February 10, 2024.**



ISBN: 979-8224900497

Written by Alexis Jones.

# Table of Contents

The Northshore Academy of Martial Arts Dojo crew. You were there when I was younger and I don't know if I would be at the place I'm at now. You guys have been my rock in the past and I love the dojo. Thank you for being there for me when I was younger and being there for me now.

Alexandru Jociva, Thank you for being a great sensei and always believing in me. If it weren't for you, I don't know if this would be possible. You have helped me through so much and continue to be there for me.

Matthew Hibbeler, Thank you for being there when I need you. We may have our ups and downs, but there is always something between us that is unbreakable. These past few years have been wonderful and I love being with you. Thank you for helping me with this book, and many more to come. There is always going to be us, and I appreciate everything you have done. I love you so much and I don't know where I would be without you.

# Chapter 1: Lost in the Wilderness

The air hung heavy with an ominous stillness as the group stumbled through the dense underbrush, their breaths creating fleeting clouds in the cold night. The remnants of what had once been a lively conversation now clung to the silence that enveloped them. The moon cast feeble rays through the thick canopy overhead, offering glimpses of twisted branches and gnarled roots that seemed to claw at the very fabric of reality. Emily, the group's de facto leader, squinted against the darkness, her eyes scanning the surroundings for any sign of familiarity. But there was none. The wilderness stretched endlessly in every direction, an impenetrable labyrinth of trees and shadows. The initial shock of their predicament had given way to a quiet, collective realization—they were truly alone, stranded in a place untouched by civilization. The echoes of the catastrophic event that had brought them here still resonated in their minds, a haunting reminder of a world forever changed.

"Are we even going in the right direction?" Jake's voice broke the uneasy quiet, his words a hesitant whisper that seemed to hang in the chilly air. He turned his gaze towards Emily, searching for reassurance that she struggled to provide.

"We have to keep moving," Emily replied, her words laced with determination. "There's bound to be a way out of this... this wilderness."

Yet, doubt lingered in the shadows, and the reality of their situation weighed heavy on each step they took. The wilderness, once an escape for those seeking solace, had become an unforgiving labyrinth, a maze of uncertainty that tested the limits of their resilience. As they ventured deeper into the unknown, the looming darkness seemed to swallow them whole, and the distant sounds of the night became an eerie symphony—an unsettling backdrop to their journey into the heart of the wilderness, where secrets lay hidden and survival was anything but guaranteed. The path ahead grew more treacherous, obscured by the thick foliage that clung to the edges of the narrow trail. The group moved in a single-file line, their senses heightened by the rustling leaves and the occasional distant howl of an unseen creature. Emily took the lead, her eyes scanning the terrain for signs of a way out.

As they trudged on, the initial shock began to give way to a simmering tension within the group. Each step deepened the imprint of uncertainty, and whispers of doubt spread like wildfire. Sarah, a young woman with a penchant for optimism, couldn't shake the feeling that they were heading in circles.

"Are we sure we're going the right way?" she asked, her voice carrying a note of worry.

Emily's determination faltered for a moment, but she quickly regained her composure. "We need to trust the path we've chosen. The longer we stay still, the more vulnerable we become."

Dusk settled over the wilderness, casting long shadows that danced in the fading light. The group, fatigued and disheartened, stumbled upon a clearing. A small, dimly lit space revealed a makeshift campsite—an unsettling discovery, as if someone had been there before them. Unease crept through the group like a shadow, but there was no time for deliberation. The encroaching darkness forced their hands, compelling them to set up a makeshift camp for the night. Tensions simmered beneath the surface as they gathered fallen branches for a meager fire, the flickering flames casting dancing shadows on their faces. Around the crackling fire, faces wore expressions of weariness and concern. Emily, realizing the fragility of their situation, sought to assert control.

"We need a plan," she declared, her eyes scanning the faces of those around her. "We can't afford to let fear dictate our actions. We'll take turns keeping watch. Safety in numbers, right?"

Nods of agreement rippled through the group, but doubt lingered in the air like an unspoken truth. As the night wore on, the flickering flames cast long shadows that danced in tandem with the secrets concealed within the wilderness. The group, though united by circumstance, faced a reality that tested the bonds of trust—a reality where survival required more than navigating the wilderness; it demanded navigating the complexities of human nature in a world turned upside down. The night deepened, and the crackling fire began to wane, casting elongated shadows that played tricks on their senses. The rhythmic sounds of nocturnal creatures intensified, echoing through the stillness of the wilderness. With each passing hour, the group's exhaustion mingled with a growing unease. Emily, wrapped in the solitude of her watch, pondered the enigma of their surroundings. A gust of wind rustled the leaves, and she felt the weight of the unknown pressing down on her shoulders. How had they ended up in this desolate place? The answers remained elusive, hidden in the shadows of a world forever altered. As the first light of dawn began to break, the others stirred from uneasy slumbers. The campsite revealed a collage of weary faces, dirt-streaked and sleep-deprived. The flickering embers of the dying fire mirrored the dwindling hope within the group.

"We can't stay here," Emily asserted, her gaze fixed on the horizon. "We need to find civilization, or at least a way to signal for help."

The group, though still grappling with uncertainty, mustered the energy to pack their meager belongings. As they resumed their journey through the dense wilderness, a collective sense of urgency hung in the air—a silent acknowledgment that their survival hinged on their ability to unravel the mysteries that surrounded them. The landscape shifted as they ventured deeper into the heart of the unknown. Thick undergrowth gave way to towering trees, their branches intertwining like guardians of ancient secrets. The terrain became more challenging, testing the limits of their endurance. The air was thick with a sense of foreboding, and each step seemed to echo a plea for answers. Yet, despite the hardships, a fragile camaraderie emerged among the group. Shared glances and silent nods spoke of an unspoken pact—a commitment to face the challenges ahead together. The wilderness, though unforgiving, became a canvas on which the bonds of survival were painted, and the group pressed on, determined to defy the odds. The mysteries of the wilderness deepened, and the group's journey took an unforeseen turn. The shadows cast by the towering trees whispered of hidden truths, waiting to be revealed as they continued their trek into the heart of the unknown.

The dense foliage gradually gave way to a clearing bathed in the soft hues of morning light. A collective sigh of relief escaped the group as they emerged from the confines of the thick forest. Before them lay a vast expanse of meadows, stretching toward the horizon like an undisturbed tapestry. Emily's gaze surveyed the open space, searching for any signs of civilization. The meadows, though serene, held an eerie quiet that amplified the solitude of their predicament. A distant mountain range loomed on the horizon, a daunting reminder that they were a mere speck in the vastness of the wilderness.

"We need a vantage point," suggested Alex, a seasoned hiker with a knack for navigation. "If we can see the lay of the land, we might spot signs of civilization or a way out of this."

The group rallied behind the idea, their weary spirits buoyed by the prospect of gaining a broader perspective. As they journeyed toward the distant mountains, a sense of determination overcame the weariness that clung to their bones. The meadows, once a seemingly endless expanse, proved to be a journey of their own. The soft earth beneath their feet gradually transformed into rocky terrain, and the air grew thinner as they ascended. The group pressed on, fueled by a mixture of hope and a shared understanding that their survival depended on pushing beyond the boundaries of their comfort. Upon reaching a crest, the landscape unfolded below them, revealing a breathtaking panorama of valleys and peaks. A hushed awe settled over the group as they took in the vastness of their surroundings. Emily's eyes scanned the horizon, searching for any signs of civilization.

"There," she exclaimed, pointing toward a distant glimmer of sunlight reflecting off what seemed to be structures. "That could be our way out."

As the group descended from the vantage point, a renewed sense of purpose infused their steps. The distant structures beckoned like beacons of hope, promising answers to the questions that lingered in the wilderness. Chapter 1, titled "Lost in the Wilderness," had begun with uncertainty and fear, but now it carried the promise of discovery and the potential for a path out of the unknown.

# Chapter 2: The Gathering Storm

The descent from the mountainous vantage point led the group toward the distant structures that shimmered in the sunlight. As they approached, the landscape transitioned from rugged wilderness to a more structured environment. Trees gave way to open spaces, and the faint murmur of a river hinted at the presence of civilization. The structures, now discernible as a cluster of buildings, stood against the backdrop of a quaint town. The sight of human habitation brought a mixture of relief and apprehension. Were the inhabitants aware of the group's presence, and how would they react to unexpected visitors? Emily, leading the way, urged caution among the group. The journey had forged a bond born out of shared challenges, but the mysteries of the wilderness had also cultivated a sense of wariness. As they entered the outskirts of the town, an unsettling quiet hung in the air. The town, though seemingly intact, felt deserted. Streets devoid of life, windows tightly shut, and an eerie silence that clung to the surroundings. The group moved cautiously, exchanging glances that mirrored the unspoken question: What had transpired here?

The main square revealed a weathered notice board with faded announcements and community events. One notice stood out—"Evacuation Point: Head to the Shelter." The words sparked a sense of urgency, a realization that the town had faced its own struggle for survival. As they delved deeper, clues unfolded like a story written in the remnants of abandoned lives. An overturned grocery cart spilled its contents across the pavement, a child's bicycle lay discarded by a doorstep, and faded murals depicted scenes of unity and resilience. A distant rumble interrupted the group's exploration. The sky, once serene, now darkened with ominous clouds that gathered on the horizon. The air carried an electric charge, and a distant thunder echoed through the town, heralding an approaching storm. Unease settled over the group as they sought shelter in the town's community center. The weathered walls seemed to absorb the weight of untold stories, and the gathering storm outside mirrored the brewing tension within the group. The town revealed itself as a canvas painted with the echoes of a past struggle. The storm, both literal and metaphorical, hinted at challenges yet to be faced. In this fragile sanctuary, the group stood on the precipice of discovery, where the secrets of the town and the mysteries of the wilderness converged.

Inside the community center, the group found a temporary respite from the encroaching storm. The atmosphere was tense as they huddled together, exchanging uncertain glances. Emily, driven by a sense of responsibility, took charge.

"We need to understand what happened here," she declared, her eyes scanning the worn-out faces of her companions. "There might be clues that can help us, and we can't afford to be caught off guard."

The group split into pairs, each assigned to investigate different areas of the community center. Dust-covered documents in the town office hinted at the hurried evacuation—emergency protocols, lists of essential supplies, and hastily drawn maps indicating a designated shelter. Meanwhile, whispers of conversation emerged among the group members, each sharing their observations and speculations. Sarah, peering through the blinds of a window, caught a glimpse of dark clouds swirling ominously.

"The storm is getting worse," she said, her voice barely audible over the distant rumble of thunder. "We should be prepared for anything."

As the group reconvened, pooling together their findings, a clearer picture began to emerge. The town had faced a catastrophic event, triggering a swift evacuation. The shelter, it seemed, held the promise of safety amidst chaos. But questions lingered. Why had the group been left unaware of this catastrophe? How had they ended up stranded in the wilderness while the town faced its own struggle for survival? Just as the group deliberated their next move, the first raindrops began to splatter against the windows. The storm, once a distant threat, now bore down on the town with relentless force. Emily, glancing at the worn evacuation notice once more, knew that answers lay beyond the walls of the community center.

"We head to the shelter," she decided, her voice cutting through the uneasy murmurs. "It's our best chance to find out what happened here and, hopefully, a way to get back to our lives."

As the group gathered their belongings and prepared to face the tempest outside, the town whispered its secrets, and the storm intensified, casting an ominous shadow over their quest for answers. In the heart of the gathering storm, the group's journey continued, propelled by the dual forces of nature and the unraveling mysteries that awaited them. The heavy door creaked open, and the group stepped out into the escalating storm. Rain lashed against them, driven by gusts of wind that seemed to carry the weight of the town's untold stories. The distant thunder roared like an echoing cry of the past, urging them forward.

With Emily at the lead, they navigated the deserted streets toward the shelter. Water pooled in the uneven cobblestone pathways, reflecting the muted glow of street lamps flickering in the turbulent wind. The town, once vibrant, now lay silent beneath the onslaught of nature. As they approached the shelter's location, a foreboding sight greeted them. The building, a sturdy structure meant to withstand the elements, bore the scars of time and neglect. Its windows, clouded with grime, revealed nothing of the sanctuary within. Emily hesitated for a moment, her eyes fixated on the shelter's entrance. The group shared a collective uncertainty, acutely aware that the answers they sought lay beyond those weathered doors. Bracing against the wind and rain, they pushed open the entrance, revealing a dimly lit interior. The air inside was heavy with the musty scent of abandonment. The flickering emergency lights cast long shadows on the walls, creating an eerie atmosphere. Silent footsteps echoed through the narrow corridors as the group explored the shelter's depths. Abandoned supplies, scattered belongings, and remnants of makeshift living spaces painted a poignant picture of the town's struggle to survive. The walls bore messages of hope and desperation, a chronicle of the emotions that had permeated these sheltered walls. In a central chamber, a large bulletin board stood, covered in faded notes, maps, and a worn-out town plan. The group gathered around it, studying the intricate web of information. It became clear that the town had faced not only the immediate threat that forced evacuation but also internal challenges—struggles for resources, conflicts, and the strain of a community pushed to its limits.

As they absorbed the weight of the shelter's history, a distant crash of thunder reminded them that the storm outside mirrored the tempest within. The group exchanged somber glances, acknowledging that their journey had only just begun. The gathering storm, both meteorological and metaphorical, had opened a door to a world of secrets, and the group stood on the threshold, uncertain of what lay ahead in this sheltered haven of revelations. The group, surrounded by the echoes of the town's struggle within the shelter, felt a growing urgency to unravel the mysteries that had brought them to this place. Emily, determined to piece together the puzzle, focused on a particularly detailed map pinned to the bulletin board.

"This map might hold the key to understanding our situation," she said, her finger tracing the worn lines and markings. "If we can decipher it, we might find clues about the events leading to our arrival here."

As the group scrutinized the map, they discovered markings indicating points of interest, evacuation routes, and potential hazards.

Cryptic notes scribbled in the margins hinted at conflicts, resource shortages, and the community's desperate attempts to survive. The realization set in that the town had faced not just a natural disaster but a complex web of challenges that strained its very fabric. Their examination was interrupted by a sudden crash outside, louder than the ongoing storm. Startled, the group rushed to the shelter's entrance, where they found debris scattered across the floor. The wind howled through the open door, and rainwater dripped from the ceiling.

"We're not alone," Jake pointed out, his gaze fixed on the disarray outside. "Something—or someone—is out there."

Emily's eyes narrowed, a mix of concern and determination in her expression. The group, now on edge, ventured cautiously into the stormy night. As they stepped outside, the wind carried hushed whispers, and shadows danced in the dim light. Through the rain-soaked streets, they glimpsed elusive figures darting between buildings. The tension rose as the group followed the fleeting shadows, navigating the labyrinth of the town in pursuit of the elusive presence. The pursuit led them to a partially concealed entrance, barely visible beneath a tangle of overgrown vines. Emily exchanged a determined look with the group, and they entered the concealed passage with a mixture of apprehension and curiosity. Inside, they found themselves in a hidden chamber—a makeshift refuge adorned with flickering candles. The walls were covered with maps, notes, and symbols. In the center stood a solitary figure, cloaked in mystery. The figure turned slowly to face them, revealing weathered features and eyes that held a mix of weariness and resilience. The air in the chamber crackled with unspoken questions, and the group, now face to face with the enigmatic guardian of secrets, braced themselves for revelations that promised to shape the trajectory of their journey in this unfamiliar world.

# Chapter 3: Ties that Bind

The hidden chamber, illuminated by flickering candlelight, bore witness to the convergence of the stranded group and the mysterious guardian. The air hung heavy with anticipation as the figures faced each other, the silence broken only by the distant rumble of thunder and the erratic patter of rain against the concealed entrance. The guardian, their identity obscured by shadows, surveyed the newcomers with a gaze that seemed to pierce through the layers of secrecy. A silent understanding passed between Emily and the cloaked figure, acknowledging the shared weight of the unknown.

"Who are you, and what happened here?" Emily's voice cut through the tension, her eyes unwavering.

The guardian, after a moment of contemplation, began to unveil a tale woven with threads of hardship and resilience. They spoke of the town's struggle against an unforeseen calamity, the fractures within the community, and the desperate quest for survival that had led to the establishment of the hidden refuge. As the narrative unfolded, the group learned of a disaster that had plunged the town into chaos. The catastrophic event, shrouded in mystery, had set off a chain reaction of challenges, from resource scarcity to internal conflicts. The guardian, a survivor forged by adversity, had taken it upon themselves to safeguard the remnants of the community. The revelation prompted a surge of questions from the group. How had the disaster affected the world beyond the town? Why were they stranded in the wilderness, oblivious to the town's struggle? The guardian's responses, though illuminating, raised more questions than answers. The intricate web of circumstances hinted at forces beyond the group's comprehension. The ties that bound them to this unfamiliar world became increasingly complex, and the enigma of their predicament deepened. As the conversation continued, the storm outside intensified, unleashing its fury upon the town. The chamber echoed with the symphony of rain, wind, and the guardian's narrative. Each word revealed not only the history of the town but also the interconnected fates of those who sought refuge within its hidden walls.

Emotions ran high among the group—awe, sympathy, and an underlying sense of solidarity. The guardian, having shared their story, looked to Emily with a gaze that spoke of mutual understanding.

"We are bound by circumstances beyond our control," the guardian acknowledged, their voice carrying the weight of a shared destiny. "To navigate the challenges ahead, we must forge new ties and unravel the mysteries that entwine us."

As the storm raged outside, the group and the guardian stood at the threshold of a new chapter—one where the ties that bound them would be tested, and the revelations yet to unfold would shape their collective journey through the unknown. The hidden chamber provided a brief respite from the storm, both within and outside its walls. As the guardian's tale unfolded, the group found themselves entangled in a narrative woven with threads of tragedy, survival, and the complexities of a world in upheaval. Emily, absorbing the weight of the revelations, realized that the ties that bound them went beyond the physical constraints of the shelter. The group and the guardian, disparate souls thrown together by circumstance, now shared a common destiny—a journey through the enigmatic tapestry of the town's struggle and the mysteries that extended beyond its borders. Determined to understand the full scope of their predicament, Emily questioned the guardian further. "How do we fit into this puzzle? Why were we stranded in the wilderness while the town faced its challenges?"

The guardian's response, though measured, carried an undercurrent of uncertainty. "Your arrival is an anomaly, an unexplained divergence from the course set by the town's collective fate. The ties that bind us may hold the answers, but their unraveling will require courage and exploration."

Outside the hidden chamber, the storm showed no signs of abating. Thunder rumbled like a distant echo of the unknown, and rain continued to beat against the shelter. The group, fortified by the revelations and a shared sense of purpose, prepared to venture back into the tempest.

"We need to explore the town further, gather clues, and understand the forces that led us here," Emily declared, her gaze resolute. "The ties that bind us may reveal our path forward."

The group, led by Emily and guided by the cryptic knowledge of the guardian, retraced their steps through the concealed entrance. As they emerged into the storm, the town awaited them, its abandoned streets a canvas on which the story of struggle and survival unfolded. Their exploration took them to forgotten corners, weathered landmarks, and remnants of the past. Each discovery added to the mosaic of the town's narrative, revealing not only its challenges but also the resilience of those who had called it home. Yet, with every step, the group sensed the presence of unseen forces at play. The ties that bound them, now more palpable than ever, seemed to guide their path, urging them deeper into the heart of the mystery that enveloped the town. As they pressed on, the storm persisted, echoing the turbulence within the group's collective journey—a journey intricately tied to the town's past and the enigmatic threads that wove their fates together. The true nature of these ties, and the challenges that lay ahead, remained concealed in the shadowy embrace of the unknown. The group, resilient against the storm and fueled by a newfound determination, explored the town with a heightened sense of purpose. Every step echoed through the deserted streets, a reminder of the interconnected destinies that had brought them to this place. In their exploration, the group uncovered remnants of what once was—a faded mural depicting the town's unity, a deserted marketplace that once buzzed with activity, and weathered signs pointing toward places of significance. Each discovery deepened the understanding of the town's history and the challenges it had faced.

As they ventured further, they reached a dilapidated town square, where a central monument stood as a silent witness to the passage of time. The monument bore inscriptions, weathered by the elements but still legible. The group gathered around, studying the words etched into the stone.

"In times of adversity, unity prevails. We are bound by the ties of our shared history and the strength that arises from our collective resilience," Emily read aloud, her voice carrying the weight of the sentiment.

The inscription resonated with the guardian's narrative—a testament to the interconnected lives of those who had called the town home. The ties that bound them, now tangible in their shared exploration, began to transcend the confines of the past and extend into the present moment. Their journey led them to a once-thriving community center, now abandoned and weatherworn. Inside, they discovered faded photographs and personal belongings left behind in haste. The artifacts painted a vivid picture of lives disrupted, yet the resilience captured in each image spoke of an enduring spirit. Amidst the artifacts, they stumbled upon an old journal—one that chronicled the daily struggles and triumphs of a resident named Maria. The pages unfolded a personal narrative, revealing the emotional highs and lows that mirrored the collective experience of the town. As they delved into Maria's entries, a realization dawned upon the group—the ties that bound them went beyond the physical confines of the shelter or the town. In the shared stories of resilience, in the echoes of a once-vibrant community, and in the fragments of lives left behind, they found a connection that transcended the bounds of time and space. The storm outside, though relentless, seemed to relent its grip as the group immersed themselves in the town's history. With each revelation, the ties that bound them tightened, weaving a narrative that intertwined their fate with the forgotten echoes of the past. As they continued their exploration, the group's shared purpose intensified—the unraveling mysteries of the town and the enigmatic ties that bound them became a collective journey, a quest for understanding in the face of the unknown. The storm, having served as both an adversary and an accomplice, echoed their footsteps as they moved toward the heart of the town's history, where the answers to their questions lay concealed.

# Chapter 4: The Calm Before

In the wake of their exploration, the group found themselves standing in the town square, surrounded by the echoes of the past. The storm, having spent its fury, retreated into a gentle drizzle, casting a serene atmosphere over the worn cobblestone pathways. The collective understanding of the town's history and the ties that bound them fostered a quiet unity among the group. The weight of the past, revealed in faded inscriptions and forgotten artifacts, became a shared burden, a narrative that connected each member to the resilient spirit of the community. As they gathered in the square, Emily, reflective and resolute, addressed the group. "We've glimpsed into the heart of this town—the struggles, the triumphs, and the ties that endure. Now, we must use this understanding to navigate the challenges that lie ahead."

The group, standing at the intersection of their own stories and the town's history, acknowledged the depth of the ties that bound them. The guardian, who had been a silent guide through the unraveling mysteries, stood alongside them, a living testament to the enduring strength of the town's spirit. Their journey, though revealing, still held unanswered questions. The anomaly of their arrival, the mysterious disaster that befell the town, and the forces at play in the larger world remained enigmatic. The calm that settled over the town square served as a brief respite—a moment to reflect, regroup, and prepare for the uncertainties that lay ahead.

"We need to find more clues, understand the true nature of our ties to this place, and unravel the mysteries that bind us," Emily declared, her gaze encompassing the faces of the group.

With a shared purpose, they embarked on the next phase of their journey. The town, once a backdrop to their struggle for survival, now became a living testament to the ties that transcended time and circumstance. Their exploration took them to forgotten corners, hidden archives, and remnants of the past that held the promise of answers. The once-deserted streets began to echo with the footsteps of those seeking understanding—the ties that bound them now propelling them forward into the unknown. As they delved deeper, the group sensed a subtle shift in the air—a calm settling over the town, a prelude to the revelations and challenges that awaited. The calm before the storm, both literal and metaphorical, hinted at a transformative moment in their collective journey—a moment where the ties that bound them would be tested, and the true nature of their connection to the town and its mysteries would be unveiled. The group's exploration led them to an old library, a repository of the town's collective knowledge and history. Dust-covered shelves lined with weathered books and faded manuscripts hinted at the passage of time. As they sifted through the archives, they uncovered records detailing the town's evolution, the events leading up to the mysterious disaster, and the resilience of its people. One particular manuscript caught Emily's attention—an ancient tome that seemed to hold the key to understanding the ties that bound them. Its pages, filled with cryptic symbols and enigmatic illustrations, spoke of a deeper connection between the town and the forces that had shaped its destiny. As the group immersed themselves in deciphering the ancient text, the atmosphere in the library shifted. A sense of anticipation hung in the air, as if the pages themselves held the power to unlock the secrets that had eluded them.

"The answers we seek may lie within these pages," Emily remarked, her eyes scanning the intricate illustrations that adorned the manuscript. "If we can unravel the mysteries encoded here, we may gain insights into the ties that bind us and the true nature of our connection to this town."

The guardian, silently observing the unfolding events, nodded in agreement. Together, they embarked on a collective effort to decipher the ancient text—a journey that required not only intellectual acumen but also an intuitive understanding of the enigmatic forces at play. As they delved into the symbols and passages, a gradual realization unfolded. The town, it seemed, was more than a mere physical location—it was an intersection of cosmic energies, a nexus where the threads of fate converged. The guardian, having experienced the town's struggles firsthand, became a living link between the past and the present. As night fell and the library's candles cast flickering shadows on the ancient manuscript, a breakthrough occurred. The symbols, once indecipherable, began to form a coherent narrative—a tale of cosmic forces, ancient prophecies, and the ties that bound the town to a destiny beyond mortal understanding. The group, now armed with newfound knowledge, emerged from the library into the night. The calm before the storm had given way to a profound revelation, and the ties that bound them had transformed from mere threads into an intricate tapestry woven with the threads of fate. Their journey, though far from over, had taken on a cosmic dimension. As they navigated the town's streets, guided by the enigmatic symbols and the guardian's understanding, they prepared to face the challenges that lay ahead—a journey that would test the limits of their newfound connections and the resilience of the ties that bound them to the cosmic forces at play.

The night enveloped the town in a quiet hush as the group, armed with the knowledge gleaned from the ancient manuscript, navigated the winding streets. The guardian, now a crucial guide in the unfolding cosmic narrative, led them toward a focal point—the town's central square. As they approached, a subtle energy permeated the air, resonating with the cosmic forces hinted at in the ancient text. Symbols etched into the cobblestones seemed to come alive under the moonlight, glowing faintly as if activated by the presence of those who sought to unravel the mysteries.

"The town is more than just a physical place; it is a convergence of cosmic energies," the guardian explained, their voice carrying the weight of ancient wisdom. "The ties that bind us go beyond our understanding of space and time. We are part of a cosmic tapestry, and our journey is intertwined with the forces that shape our destiny."

The group, now attuned to the cosmic resonance surrounding them, stood in the central square, where an ancient altar stood—a nexus of energy that bridged the gap between the earthly realm and the cosmic forces at play. Emily, empowered by the collective knowledge and the ties that bound them, approached the altar. Symbols on its surface matched those in the ancient manuscript, creating a connection that seemed to transcend the physical world. As the group gathered around, a surge of energy pulsed through the town, resonating with the cosmic forces. The symbols on the altar glowed brighter, casting an ethereal light that bathed the square in a celestial glow. The guardian, with a solemn demeanor, spoke words that echoed with ancient resonance, awakening the latent energies within. A portal, unseen by mortal eyes, began to manifest—a bridge between the earthly realm and the cosmic forces that governed the town's destiny. The group, now standing at the threshold of the unknown, faced a choice—to step through the portal and embrace the cosmic journey or to remain anchored in the familiar confines of the town. The cosmic forces, now awakened, seemed to beckon them toward a path of discovery and revelation. The ties that bound them, once enigmatic threads, now pulsed with a cosmic energy that transcended the ordinary boundaries of their existence. As the group contemplated their next move, the guardian turned to them with a gaze that held a mixture of wisdom and anticipation. The cosmic journey, with its promise of answers and challenges, awaited those who dared to step beyond the threshold—a journey that would test the resilience of the ties that bound them to the cosmic forces that shaped their fate. The group stood at the threshold of the cosmic portal, the celestial glow illuminating their faces with a surreal luminescence. The ancient symbols on the altar pulsed in harmony with the cosmic energies, inviting them to embark on a journey that transcended the boundaries of their understanding. Emily, the guardian, and the rest of the group exchanged glances, a silent acknowledgment passing between them. The ties that bound them, strengthened by shared experiences and the unraveling mysteries, had brought them to this pivotal moment—the choice between the known and the cosmic unknown.

"The cosmic forces are intertwined with our destiny," the guardian intoned, their voice carrying the weight of ages. "To truly understand the ties that bind us and the mysteries that surround this town, we must venture beyond the confines of the familiar."

With a collective breath, the group made the decision to step through the cosmic portal. As they crossed the threshold, the world around them blurred, and a sense of weightlessness enveloped them. The transition was both physical and metaphysical, a journey through the cosmic fabric that wove the threads of their existence. As they emerged on the other side, the landscape transformed into an otherworldly realm—an astral plane where the cosmic forces manifested in vibrant hues. Celestial constellations danced overhead, and ethereal energies pulsed through the air. The guardian, now a beacon of ancient wisdom, guided them through this celestial landscape. They explained that the town's destiny was intricately connected to cosmic energies, and the group's arrival had triggered a convergence of forces that defied mortal comprehension.

"This journey is not just about unraveling the mysteries of the town," the guardian explained. "It is about understanding the cosmic ties that bind us to the intricate web of existence."

As they traversed the astral plane, the group encountered visions that transcended time and space. They witnessed the town's inception, its struggles, and the moments of triumph that echoed through the cosmic tapestry. The ties that bound them became threads woven into the very fabric of the cosmos. Yet, amidst the cosmic revelations, challenges emerged—trials that tested the group's unity, resilience, and understanding of the cosmic forces. The guardian, a stalwart guide, encouraged them to navigate the astral challenges with the strength derived from their shared experiences. The cosmic journey, though profound and mysterious, carried the promise of enlightenment. As the group pressed on, guided by the guardian and propelled by the cosmic forces, they faced the unknown with a newfound sense of purpose—the ties that bound them now extending beyond the earthly realm into the vast expanse of the cosmos. As they ventured deeper into the astral plane, the mysteries unfolded, and the true nature of their cosmic connection became increasingly clear. The calm before the storm had given way to a celestial odyssey, where the group's journey through the unknown was intricately woven into the cosmic design that shaped their destiny.

In the heart of the astral plane, the group encountered celestial phenomena that transcended mortal understanding. The cosmic forces, guided by the guardian, unveiled visions that portrayed the interconnected fate of the town and its inhabitants with the cosmic tapestry. As they traversed the astral landscape, symbols and images began to form a coherent narrative—a cosmic tale that revealed the profound relationship between the town and the celestial energies. It became evident that the group's presence in the town and their subsequent journey through the astral plane were not random occurrences but integral threads woven into the cosmic design. The guardian, now a conduit of ancient wisdom, spoke of a cosmic alignment that occurred once in ages—a convergence of forces that held the power to reshape destinies. The group, bound by the ties that had brought them together, found themselves at the epicenter of this cosmic event.

"The town's fate and your arrival were not mere chance," the guardian explained. "You are catalysts in a cosmic experiment, players in a grand design that seeks to harmonize the energies of the earthly realm with the celestial forces that govern the cosmos."

As the group embraced their role in this cosmic drama, they faced trials that tested their bonds and individual strengths. Ethereal entities, embodiments of cosmic energy, presented challenges that required collaboration, resilience, and an understanding of the ties that bound them. With each trial overcome, the group felt a surge of cosmic energy coursing through them—an enlightenment that went beyond mere mortal comprehension. The astral plane, once an enigmatic realm, became a canvas on which the group's journey unfolded—a journey intimately connected to the cosmic dance of forces. As they neared the culmination of their astral odyssey, the guardian led them to a focal point—an ethereal gateway that pulsed with celestial brilliance. It marked the threshold between the astral plane and the earthly realm, a symbolic transition between the cosmic forces and the town that had served as their vessel. Standing before the gateway, the group felt the convergence of energies intensify. The ties that bound them, now interwoven with the cosmic threads, resonated with a newfound harmony. The guardian, their purpose fulfilled, conveyed a final piece of cosmic wisdom.

"The journey through the astral plane has unveiled the cosmic ties that bind you to the town and the forces that govern your destinies. As you step through the gateway, you will return to the earthly realm, carrying with you the enlightenment gained from the cosmic journey."

With collective resolve, the group approached the gateway. As they crossed back into the earthly realm, the astral plane's brilliance faded, leaving them standing in the town square—the nexus of cosmic forces that had shaped their destinies. The guardian, now a figure of quiet reverence, conveyed a parting message. "The ties that bind you are now intertwined with the cosmic design. Embrace the knowledge gained, for your journey through the unknown has just begun."

As the astral gateway closed behind them, the group stood in the town square, renewed and enlightened. The calm that enveloped the town held a different resonance, a quiet acknowledgment of the profound ties that bound them to the cosmic forces that shaped their existence. The mysteries had unraveled, and the group, now bearing the cosmic enlightenment, prepared to face the earthly realm with a clarity that transcended the ordinary boundaries of understanding.

# Chapter 5: First Ripples of Discord

The return from the astral plane left the group in a state of cosmic enlightenment, their minds pulsating with the resonance of the celestial journey. As they stood in the town square, the guardian's parting words echoed in their thoughts—the ties that bound them had transcended the earthly realm, and a newfound clarity accompanied their return. However, the serenity that lingered in the air was soon disrupted by subtle ripples of discord. The group, now more attuned to the cosmic energies, sensed a disturbance that went beyond the physical realm. The town, once a haven of mystery, now whispered of unseen tensions that lay beneath the surface. Emily, ever vigilant, perceived the first signs of discord among the group members. A subtle shift in dynamics, the emergence of unspoken doubts, and the traces of cosmic enlightenment casting shadows of uncertainty—all hinted at the challenges that awaited them.

"The cosmic journey has changed us," Emily acknowledged, addressing the group with a mix of contemplation and concern. "The ties that bind us have taken on a cosmic dimension, but with that comes the responsibility of understanding and navigating the unseen forces at play."

As they ventured into the town, the first ripples of discord manifested in unexpected ways. Seemingly trivial disagreements escalated, and shadows of doubt cast fleeting shadows over the once-unified group. The cosmic enlightenment, while empowering, had also opened a gateway to unexplored facets of their own minds. In their interactions, the group members grappled with the complexities of the newfound cosmic ties. The town, a reflection of their interconnected destinies, now served as a testing ground for the resilience of these ties. Unspoken fears, aspirations, and conflicting perspectives emerged, challenging the unity that had carried them through the trials of the astral plane. Amidst the subtle discord, the guardian's absence loomed. The cosmic figure, a source of guidance and wisdom, had fulfilled its purpose, leaving the group to navigate the earthly realm and its challenges on their own. The question of their continued cohesion in the face of cosmic enlightenment remained unanswered. As tensions simmered and the first ripples of discord echoed through the town, Emily took on the mantle of leadership with a determination to preserve the ties that had brought them this far. The cosmic journey, though enlightening, had also laid bare the complexities of their interconnected fates. The town, once a tapestry of mystery, now became a battleground where the group's resilience would be tested. The cosmic ties, both a source of strength and a potential source of conflict, set the stage for a new chapter—a chapter where the group would grapple with the first ripples of discord and the challenges of understanding the cosmic forces that bound them together.

Emily, sensing the growing tensions within the group, called for a gathering in the town square. The echoes of cosmic enlightenment still resonated in their minds, but the shadows of discord threatened to overshadow the newfound clarity.

"Let's not allow these ripples of discord to fracture the ties that bind us," Emily addressed the group with a measured tone, her eyes scanning the faces of her companions. "The cosmic journey has granted us understanding, but it also demands our unity in the face of challenges."

The group, now acutely aware of the subtle fractures in their camaraderie, engaged in an open dialogue. Unspoken concerns were voiced, and conflicting perspectives came to the forefront. The cosmic enlightenment, it seemed, had ignited a spark of individualism that needed to be harmonized with the collective understanding gained from the astral journey. As the discussions unfolded, a realization dawned—the ties that bound them were not immune to the complexities of human emotions. Cosmic enlightenment, while transformative, did not exempt them from the vulnerabilities that defined their shared humanity. With a collective commitment to understanding and respect, the group embarked on a journey of introspection. They delved into the depths of their own cosmic enlightenment, seeking to align individual perspectives with the cosmic tapestry that connected them. Amidst the ongoing dialogue, a series of incidents highlighted the need for balance. Minor disagreements escalated into moments of tension, and the town, once a symbol of mystery, now mirrored the internal struggles of the group. In their quest for harmony, the group revisited the town's landmarks, drawing strength from the ties that had shaped their journey. The guardian's parting words resonated—the cosmic ties required not just understanding but a conscious effort to transcend individual differences. As they navigated the town's labyrinth of history, the group encountered symbolic challenges that mirrored the internal discord. Together, they faced trials that tested their unity, resilience, and commitment to the cosmic journey. Each challenge, though rooted in the earthly realm, held cosmic significance—a reflection of the ties that bound them both to the town and the celestial forces.

Through introspection and collective effort, the group began to restore harmony. The first ripples of discord, though inevitable, became catalysts for a deeper understanding of the cosmic ties. In the town square, where cosmic enlightenment had initially cast its glow, the group found a renewed sense of unity—a unity forged not only through shared experiences but through the acknowledgment of individual strengths and perspectives. As the echoes of cosmic discord subsided, the group stood together, their ties now strengthened by the trials they had faced. The town, once a backdrop to mystery, had become a crucible of transformation. The cosmic journey, with its challenges and revelations, had set the stage for the group's continued exploration—a journey that went beyond the astral plane and into the uncharted territories of the unknown. The renewed unity within the group, forged through the trials of discord, became a source of strength as they ventured further into the town. The cosmic ties, once tested, now resonated with a harmonious energy that transcended individual differences. The group, aware of the delicate balance required to navigate the cosmic journey, approached their challenges with a newfound understanding. Their exploration led them to a forgotten chamber beneath the town—an ancient sanctum steeped in cosmic symbolism. Symbols on the walls told a story of cosmic cycles, celestial alignments, and the interplay of forces that governed the town's destiny. It was here that they encountered a celestial artifact—a manifestation of the cosmic energies that had shaped their journey. The artifact pulsed with an otherworldly glow, resonating with the harmonized cosmic ties of the group. As they approached, the artifact unveiled visions that transcended time and space—moments from the town's past, present, and potential futures unfolded in a celestial dance. Emily, captivated by the cosmic revelations, recognized the significance of their journey.

"The ties that bind us have the power to shape not only our destinies but also the fate of the town and the cosmic forces at play."

THE GROUP, STANDING amidst the cosmic echoes, felt a shared responsibility to navigate the earthly realm with wisdom gained from the astral journey. The sanctum, a nexus of cosmic energies, became a focal point for reflection and communion—a place where the group could harness the power of their intertwined destinies. As they lingered in the sanctum, the cosmic artifact bestowed upon them a celestial gift—a heightened awareness that allowed them to perceive the subtle energies of the town and the cosmic forces that governed it. The group, now attuned to the ebb and flow of the cosmic currents, set out to explore the town with a renewed purpose. Their journey took them to forgotten corners and hidden passages where the town's mysteries unfolded. Cosmic symbols, once cryptic, now revealed their significance, guiding the group toward revelations that went beyond the earthly realm. With each discovery, the group's cosmic ties strengthened, anchoring them in a shared understanding of their intertwined destinies. As they navigated the town's labyrinth, they encountered remnants of cosmic rituals and ancient ceremonies that spoke of a deep connection between the earthly and celestial realms. The guardian's parting words echoed—the ties that bound them were not merely threads of fate but conduits through which cosmic energies flowed. In their exploration, the group discovered a celestial observatory—a place where the cosmic forces could be observed in their intricate dance. Symbols aligned with celestial constellations adorned the observatory, offering glimpses into the cosmic patterns that governed the town's destiny.

Standing beneath the celestial canopy, the group experienced a moment of transcendence—a communion with the cosmic energies that pulsed through the town. The ties that bound them became conduits for the celestial forces, and in that moment, they realized the profound impact their journey would have on the cosmic design. As they left the observatory, the group carried with them the cosmic resonance of their shared experience. The town, once a tapestry of mystery, now embraced them as stewards of the cosmic ties that bound its destiny. The journey, far from over, continued with a clarity that went beyond the earthly realm—a journey where the group's cosmic ties would shape not only their individual fates but the very fabric of the town and the celestial forces that guided its existence. Guided by the celestial resonance within them, the group pressed on, their cosmic ties becoming a guiding force in their exploration of the town. Symbols and cosmic energies intertwined with their earthly surroundings, revealing hidden paths and forgotten chambers that held the keys to the town's cosmic destiny.

In their journey, they stumbled upon an ancient amphitheater—a place where cosmic rituals were once performed to align the town with celestial forces. The remnants of cosmic symbols adorned the amphitheater's stage, each marking a connection between the earthly realm and the cosmic tapestry. As they stood in the center of the amphitheater, the group felt a surge of cosmic energy, resonating with the celestial frequencies. Symbols beneath their feet glowed with an ethereal light, echoing the harmony of their intertwined destinies. The guardian's wisdom echoed—the town's fate and their cosmic ties were intricately linked. In this sacred space, the group communed with the cosmic energies, channeling the resonance within themselves. Visions of the town's past, present, and potential futures played out before them in a cosmic tableau. The ties that bound them, now heightened by the celestial energies, granted them insights into the town's unfolding cosmic narrative.

"The town's destiny is interwoven with the cosmic forces, and our journey is a dance within this grand design," Emily proclaimed, acknowledging the profound connection they shared.

As they delved deeper into the cosmic mysteries, the group uncovered an ancient cosmic clock—a celestial mechanism that measured the ebb and flow of cosmic energies within the town. The clock's intricate gears and symbols depicted the cyclical nature of their journey, marking moments of cosmic alignment and the convergence of destinies. The guardian's presence, though absent in the physical form, lingered in the cosmic echoes of the town. The group, now stewards of the cosmic ties, understood the responsibility that came with their heightened awareness. They vowed to preserve the delicate balance between the earthly and celestial realms, embracing the cosmic journey with reverence. As they explored further, the group encountered a cosmic nexus—an ethereal chamber where the threads of fate converged. Here, the ties that bound them became tangible, visible threads woven into the cosmic tapestry. Each member saw their own thread entwined with others, creating a pattern that reflected the shared experiences and cosmic resonance. In the nexus, the group glimpsed the town's cosmic potential—an evolving tapestry influenced by their actions and choices. The threads of fate, though interconnected, allowed for individual expression, highlighting the delicate interplay between unity and diversity within the cosmic design. Leaving the cosmic nexus, the group emerged into the town square, where the cosmic energies resonated with a renewed intensity. The ties that bound them, now illuminated by the cosmic journey, held the power to shape the town's destiny. The guardian's parting words echoed once more, a reminder that their journey was a continuation of the cosmic dance—an exploration of the celestial forces that guided their interconnected destinies.

As they stood in the town square, the group felt the weight of their cosmic ties—a responsibility to navigate the earthly and celestial realms with wisdom and unity. The journey, marked by cosmic enlightenment and the trials of discord, continued with a profound sense of purpose—a purpose woven into the very fabric of the town's cosmic narrative. The cosmic energies in the town square pulsed with a renewed vitality as the group, now stewards of the celestial ties that bound them, contemplated their next steps. The cosmic journey, with its revelations and challenges, had transformed the group's perception of their interconnected destinies, aligning them with the celestial forces that guided the town's cosmic narrative.

As they prepared to venture further, Emily addressed the group with a sense of determination. "Our cosmic ties have granted us insight and responsibility. We must use this newfound understanding to navigate the complexities of the town's cosmic design. Our actions have the power to shape not only our destinies but the very fabric of the celestial forces at play."

The group, united by a shared sense of purpose, embarked on a journey that intertwined earthly exploration with cosmic awareness. Symbols and cosmic energies guided them through the town, revealing hidden chambers and forgotten lore that added layers to the unfolding cosmic tapestry. In their exploration, they encountered celestial anomalies—places where the cosmic energies fluctuated, hinting at the intricate dance between the earthly and celestial realms. These anomalies held the potential for revelations, challenging the group to decipher their significance and harmonize the energies within. As they faced celestial trials, the group's understanding of their cosmic ties deepened. Each challenge brought them closer to the essence of the town's cosmic design, demanding not only unity but also an attunement to the subtle currents of celestial energy that shaped their journey. Amidst the cosmic anomalies, the group stumbled upon an ancient celestial well—a source of cosmic energies that had nourished the town's connection with the celestial forces for centuries. The guardian's wisdom resonated in the echoes of the well, emphasizing the importance of preserving the delicate balance between the earthly and celestial realms. As they gathered around the celestial well, the group communed with the cosmic energies, drawing strength from the ties that bound them. Visions of the town's past, present, and potential futures played out in the ripples of the well, offering glimpses into the cosmic tapestry that continued to unfold.

"The cosmic well is a reflection of our shared journey, a reservoir of energies that transcend the boundaries of time and space," Emily remarked, acknowledging the profound connection they had with the celestial forces.

With a renewed sense of purpose, the group continued their exploration. The town, now a living embodiment of cosmic harmony, responded to their attunement with celestial energies. Symbols glowed with ethereal light, guiding them toward the heart of the cosmic design that governed their destinies. As they approached the town's cosmic nexus once again, the threads of fate became more intricate, weaving together the collective experiences and cosmic resonance of the group. The celestial energies pulsed with a rhythmic cadence, indicating moments of cosmic alignment that would shape the town's destiny. In the cosmic nexus, the group faced a pivotal choice—a decision that would send ripples through the celestial currents and influence the town's cosmic narrative. The ties that bound them, now empowered by cosmic enlightenment, compelled them to make choices that harmonized with the intricate dance of fate. As they stood at the precipice of the cosmic nexus, the group understood the weight of their decisions. The cosmic journey, marked by revelations, trials, and harmonious communion with celestial forces, had brought them to a crossroads where the earthly and cosmic realms converged. With a collective breath, the group embraced their role as custodians of the cosmic ties, ready to navigate the cosmic nexus and shape the destiny of the town. The celestial energies, now attuned to their purpose, awaited the choices that would echo through the cosmic tapestry, leaving an indelible mark on the interconnected destinies of the group and the celestial forces that guided their cosmic journey.

The group entered the cosmic nexus with a collective understanding that their choices in this pivotal moment would reverberate through the celestial forces governing the town's destiny. Symbols and cosmic energies surrounded them, weaving an intricate dance that reflected the interconnected threads of fate. In the heart of the cosmic nexus, the group encountered a celestial scale—an ethereal balance that symbolized the delicate equilibrium between earthly actions and cosmic repercussions. Symbols representing their choices shimmered on one side of the scale, while the other side awaited the cosmic responses that would unfold. Emily, as the de facto leader, faced the cosmic scale with a sense of gravity. "Our choices here will shape the town's cosmic narrative. Let us consider each decision with reverence for the ties that bind us and the celestial forces at play."

The group, guided by the wisdom gained from their cosmic journey, deliberated on the symbols representing various aspects of their journey—the trials faced, the cosmic enlightenment attained, and the unity that had emerged from the trials of discord. Each choice held the potential to influence the town's cosmic resonance, and the group navigated the cosmic scale with a blend of intuition and reflection. As the symbols were placed on the scale, the celestial energies responded with subtle shifts. The cosmic dance intensified, and the threads of fate vibrated with an intricate resonance. The group witnessed visions of the town's potential futures—each choice echoing through the cosmic tapestry, shaping the destiny of the town and the celestial forces. The guardian's presence, though no longer visible, lingered in the cosmic nexus. The group, now the architects of the town's cosmic narrative, felt the weight of their responsibilities. The ties that bound them became conduits for the celestial forces, allowing the group to guide the town toward a harmonious alignment with the cosmic design. As the last symbol found its place on the scale, a celestial glow enveloped the cosmic nexus. The group, attuned to the cosmic energies, sensed a profound shift in the town's destiny. The cosmic forces responded to the choices made, weaving a narrative that resonated with the group's unity, cosmic enlightenment, and the trials that had shaped their journey.

The cosmic nexus, now aglow with ethereal light, conveyed a sense of cosmic satisfaction. The group, having embraced their role as custodians of the cosmic ties, stepped away from the celestial scale with a mixture of awe and reverence. As they exited the cosmic nexus, the town seemed to breathe with a renewed energy. Symbols and cosmic energies radiated with a harmonious resonance, echoing the choices made in the cosmic nexus. The group, now more deeply entwined with the celestial forces, prepared to continue their exploration with a sense of purpose—an understanding that their journey, though cosmic in nature, was an ongoing dance within the grand design of the town's interconnected destinies. The cosmic ties, once tested by discord and harmonized through enlightenment, now pulsed with a transcendent energy. The group, their earthly and cosmic selves inextricably linked, moved forward with a clarity that transcended the ordinary boundaries of understanding. The town, forever shaped by their choices, awaited the unfolding of the cosmic narrative that would define the next chapter in their interconnected destinies.

With the cosmic nexus behind them, the group ventured deeper into the town, the celestial energies now in harmonious resonance with the choices made at the heart of the cosmic design. Symbols and cosmic threads guided them toward a newfound understanding of their interconnected destinies and the evolving tapestry of the town's cosmic narrative. As they explored, the group encountered a cosmic observatory—the celestial counterpart to the earthly observatory they had previously discovered. Symbols aligned with constellations adorned the walls, and an ethereal glow bathed the room in celestial light. The observatory, a bridge between the earthly and cosmic realms, offered a vantage point to witness the cosmic dance of forces. Gazing through the celestial telescope, the group beheld visions of distant constellations and cosmic phenomena. The celestial forces, now attuned to their choices, unveiled secrets of the broader cosmic tapestry, connecting the town to a larger cosmic narrative that spanned galaxies and dimensions.

"The town's destiny is intertwined with the cosmos itself," Emily mused, her eyes fixed on the celestial wonders. "Our journey, though rooted in the earthly realm, has far-reaching implications in the grand design of the universe."

As they left the observatory, the group sensed a cosmic current guiding them toward a monumental cosmic portal—a gateway that transcended the earthly boundaries and led to the cosmic realms beyond. The ties that bound them pulsed with anticipation as they approached the ethereal gateway, symbols glowing in response to their celestial attunement. With collective resolve, the group crossed the cosmic threshold, stepping into an astral expanse where cosmic energies manifested in vivid hues. The guardian's presence, though absent in physical form, lingered as a guiding force in the astral realm, connecting the group to the cosmic forces that governed their destinies. The astral journey unfolded with surreal landscapes and celestial phenomena, each representing facets of the cosmic design. Ethereal entities, embodiments of cosmic energies, guided the group through trials that tested their unity, wisdom, and attunement to the cosmic currents. As they navigated the astral plane, the group encountered visions of their past, present, and potential futures. Cosmic revelations unfolded, revealing the threads of fate that bound them to the celestial forces. The group, now seasoned travelers of the cosmic realms, embraced the astral odyssey with a sense of purpose—a determination to unravel the mysteries that transcended the boundaries of the earthly realm. Amidst the cosmic wonders, the group faced challenges that required not only unity but a deep understanding of the cosmic energies at play. Symbols and celestial patterns guided them through the astral trials, each challenge a reflection of the choices made in the cosmic nexus and their continued journey within the grand design of the town's interconnected destinies. As they traversed the astral realms, the group's cosmic ties strengthened, resonating with the celestial energies that pulsed through the cosmos. The guardian, a guiding presence in spirit, encouraged them to embrace the cosmic forces with humility and reverence, for they were not merely participants in the cosmic dance but stewards of the town's interconnected destinies.

The astral journey, though filled with challenges, carried the promise of deeper cosmic understanding. The group, now attuned to the celestial forces, pressed on with unwavering determination, eager to uncover the cosmic mysteries that awaited them in the vast expanse of the astral plane. As the group continued their astral odyssey, the ties that bound them became conduits for the cosmic energies, weaving a narrative that transcended the earthly realm. The mysteries of the astral plane unfolded, and the group, now cosmic travelers, prepared to face the challenges and revelations that lay ahead in their ongoing exploration of the interconnected destinies that shaped the town and the cosmic forces that guided its existence.

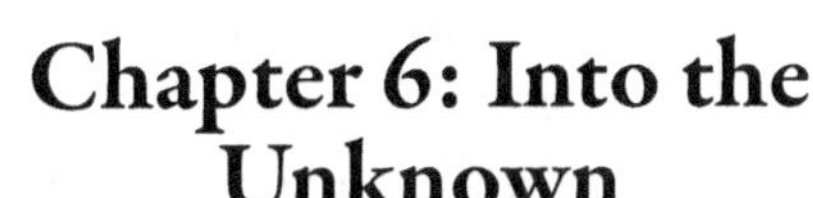

# Chapter 6: Into the Unknown

The astral journey unfolded, and the group found themselves traversing through the vast expanse of the cosmic realms, guided by the ethereal glow of celestial energies. Symbols and cosmic patterns illuminated their path as they ventured deeper into the unknown territories of the astral plane. The guardian's words echoed in their minds, urging them to embrace the cosmic forces with an open heart and a keen understanding. The group, now seasoned travelers of the astral realms, faced challenges that transcended the earthly boundaries, testing the resilience of their cosmic ties and the depth of their attunement to the celestial currents. As they continued through the astral plane, the group encountered astral gateways—portals to dimensions beyond their comprehension. Each gateway presented a choice, a decision that would influence not only their individual fates but the cosmic narrative that unfolded around them. Symbols etched into the astral gateways shimmered with cosmic significance, offering glimpses into potential futures and alternate realities. The group deliberated on each choice, considering the cosmic threads that bound them and the profound impact their decisions could have on the interconnected destinies of the town and the celestial forces. With each astral gateway traversed, the group found themselves in surreal landscapes that defied earthly logic. Celestial landscapes unfolded—vibrant realms where cosmic energies danced in intricate patterns, reflecting the interconnected threads of fate that guided their journey.

In the heart of the astral realms, the group encountered a cosmic council—an assembly of celestial beings who held ancient wisdom and knowledge of the cosmic design. The council, luminous and ethereal, greeted the group with a recognition of their attunement to the celestial forces.

"The ties that bind you are conduits of cosmic energy," spoke a celestial being, their voice resonating with cosmic echoes. "Your journey is a testament to the interconnected destinies that shape the town and the grand design of the cosmic tapestry."

The council imparted cosmic wisdom, revealing the intricate connections between earthly actions and celestial repercussions. They spoke of cosmic cycles, celestial alignments, and the eternal dance of forces that shaped the destinies of not only the town but the entire cosmos. Empowered by the celestial knowledge bestowed upon them, the group continued their astral odyssey. Symbols and cosmic energies guided them through astral challenges that demanded not only unity but a profound understanding of the cosmic forces at play. As they approached the cosmic apex of their journey, the group stood before a celestial gateway—a portal that led to the heart of the cosmic tapestry. Symbols on the gateway pulsed with cosmic energy, and the group, now attuned to the celestial currents, prepared to step into the unknown realms that awaited them. With collective resolve, they crossed the celestial threshold, leaving behind the astral plane and entering a dimension where the boundaries between the earthly and cosmic realms blurred. The cosmic forces, now more palpable than ever, beckoned them to explore the mysteries that lay within the heart of the cosmic tapestry. And so, as the group ventured further into the unknown, their cosmic ties intertwined with the celestial energies that governed the cosmos. The guardian's guidance, though no longer in a visible form, echoed in the cosmic currents, guiding them through the uncharted territories of the cosmic realms. The journey into the unknown had begun, and the group, now cosmic travelers, embraced the mysteries that awaited them in the intricate dance of the interconnected destinies that shaped both the town and the vast expanse of the cosmos.

In the heart of the cosmic tapestry, the group found themselves surrounded by celestial wonders that transcended mortal imagination. Ethereal landscapes unfolded, where cosmic energies pulsed with vibrant hues, and celestial entities drifted in a harmonious dance. Symbols adorned the astral terrain, revealing glimpses of the interconnected destinies that wove together the earthly and cosmic realms. The cosmic tapestry, a manifestation of the town's interconnected fates, guided the group toward monumental cosmic structures—a celestial library that housed the accumulated knowledge of ages, an observatory that observed the cosmic dance of galaxies, and an ethereal temple where cosmic energies resonated in sacred harmony. As they explored these celestial landmarks, the group delved into the profound wisdom embedded in the cosmic tapestry. Symbols revealed the histories of celestial alignments that had shaped the town's destiny, and cosmic visions depicted potential futures influenced by the choices made within the astral realms. In the celestial library, ancient tomes whispered cosmic secrets, unveiling the intricate connections between the earthly and cosmic forces. The group, their cosmic ties resonating with celestial energies, absorbed the cosmic knowledge that transcended the boundaries of mortal understanding. The observatory offered a panoramic view of cosmic constellations, each symbolizing a unique aspect of the town's destiny. As the group gazed into the astral expanse, they recognized patterns that mirrored their journey—a cosmic dance that echoed the trials, revelations, and choices made within the interconnected destinies of the town. In the ethereal temple, the group encountered cosmic guardians—celestial beings who bore witness to the unfolding tapestry of destinies. The guardians spoke in cosmic echoes, conveying the significance of the group's journey and the responsibility that came with their attunement to the celestial forces.

"The ties that bind you are threads in the cosmic fabric, woven into the very essence of the universe," spoke a celestial guardian. "Your journey, guided by the cosmic currents, has brought you to the heart of the cosmic tapestry. Here, the destinies of the town and the cosmos converge."

As the group communed with the celestial guardians, symbols and cosmic energies merged in a harmonious symphony, creating a resonance that echoed through the cosmic tapestry. The guardian's guidance, though now a collective echo within the group's cosmic ties, guided them toward a cosmic nexus—the nexus of destinies where the threads of fate converged. In the cosmic nexus, the group encountered a cosmic entity—a manifestation of the town's collective consciousness and the celestial forces that governed its destiny. The entity, luminous and enigmatic, acknowledged the group's presence with a cosmic resonance that transcended words.

"You are the stewards of the interconnected destinies that shape the town and the cosmos," intoned the cosmic entity. "Your journey, marked by trials, enlightenment, and choices, has led you to the nexus of destinies. Here, the threads of fate are woven into the cosmic tapestry with the guidance of your cosmic ties."

The group, now custodians of the town's destiny, faced a cosmic choice within the nexus of destinies. Symbols representing potential futures and celestial alignments shimmered with significance. The group deliberated, their decisions echoing through the cosmic tapestry and influencing the town's destiny in profound ways. As symbols found their place within the cosmic nexus, the celestial energies responded with a symphony of cosmic harmonies. The group witnessed visions of the town's potential futures, each influenced by the choices made within the nexus of destinies. With the cosmic choice made, the group emerged from the cosmic nexus, their cosmic ties now intertwined with the town's destiny on a cosmic level. The guardian's echo, though soft, resonated in the astral expanse, acknowledging the group's role as cosmic travelers and custodians of the interconnected destinies that shaped the town and the cosmos. The group, guided by their cosmic ties and the wisdom gained from the astral and celestial realms, prepared to continue their journey. The mysteries of the cosmic tapestry unfolded before them, and the interconnected destinies of the town and the celestial forces beckoned them to explore the uncharted territories that lay beyond the known realms of the earthly and cosmic realms. And so, as they stepped into the astral expanse once again, the group embraced the unknown with a sense of purpose and reverence. The guardian's guidance, now an eternal echo in the cosmic currents, accompanied them as they ventured further into the vast expanse of the interconnected destinies that shaped both the town and the boundless cosmos. The journey into the unknown continued, guided by the cosmic ties that bound them to the intricate dance of destinies within the cosmic tapestry.

The group, now propelled by cosmic ties and guided by the guardian's ethereal echo, ventured deeper into the uncharted territories of the interconnected destinies that shaped both the town and the boundless cosmos. The astral expanse unfolded before them, a canvas of celestial energies and symbols that hinted at the mysteries yet to be unveiled. As they traversed the cosmic realms, the group encountered celestial anomalies—pockets of energy that resonated with the echoes of their choices within the cosmic nexus. These anomalies, glowing with ethereal light, offered glimpses into potential paths that diverged from the known trajectory of the town's destiny. Symbols etched into the cosmic energies guided them toward a cosmic crossroads—a nexus of potential futures where the threads of fate intertwined in intricate patterns. The group, now adept at navigating the celestial currents, faced choices that would shape not only the town's destiny but also the cosmic narrative that extended far beyond the earthly realm. With each cosmic crossroads traversed, the group experienced visions of alternate realities and potential outcomes influenced by their decisions. The guardian's echo resonated, encouraging them to consider the interconnected destinies that stretched across the vast expanse of the cosmos. In one cosmic path, the group witnessed a future where the town became a beacon of cosmic enlightenment, its residents attuned to celestial energies that harmonized with the cosmic forces. Symbols of unity and cosmic awareness adorned the astral landscapes, reflecting the choices made within the cosmic nexus. In another path, the group glimpsed a reality where discord among the townspeople intensified, casting shadows over the celestial energies. Symbols of dissonance and cosmic imbalance pulsed through the astral expanse, emphasizing the consequences of choices that strayed from the cosmic harmony.

As the group explored these potential futures, they realized the delicate balance between earthly actions and cosmic repercussions. The cosmic ties that bound them became conduits for the energies that shaped destinies, and the responsibility of stewarding the interconnected fates weighed heavily on their ethereal journey. The guardian's echo guided them to a celestial convergence—a nexus of cosmic energies that merged with the town's destiny in a symphony of ethereal light. Symbols representing the group's choices illuminated the astral expanse, intertwining with the celestial forces that governed the town and the cosmic realms. In this cosmic convergence, the group faced a final cosmic choice—a decision that would echo through the interconnected destinies and resonate with the very fabric of the celestial forces. Symbols shimmered with cosmic significance, and the group, attuned to the celestial currents, deliberated with a deep understanding of the profound impact their choices would have. As the symbols found their place within the cosmic convergence, a transcendent glow enveloped the group. The ethereal light pulsed through the astral expanse, and the celestial energies responded with a harmonious resonance that echoed the group's choices.

The guardian's echo, though subtle, expressed cosmic satisfaction as the group emerged from the cosmic convergence. The interconnected destinies, now shaped by the ethereal choices made within the cosmic tapestry, unfolded before them in a grand tableau of celestial energies. With a renewed sense of purpose, the group continued their astral journey, guided by the cosmic ties that bound them to the intricacies of the interconnected destinies. The town, forever entwined with the cosmic forces, awaited the unfolding of a narrative that stretched beyond the boundaries of mortal understanding. As the group traversed the celestial currents, the guardian's echo whispered of cosmic revelations yet to come. The mysteries of the interconnected destinies, woven into the fabric of the cosmic tapestry, beckoned them to explore the uncharted territories that lay beyond the known realms of the earthly and cosmic dimensions. And so, with each step in the astral expanse, the group embraced the ongoing journey into the unknown—a journey marked by cosmic ties, celestial guidance, and the profound interconnected destinies that shaped not only the town but the vast and boundless cosmos. The ethereal echoes of the guardian resonated in the cosmic currents, a guiding force that propelled them further into the mysteries that awaited them in the intricate dance of destinies within the cosmic tapestry.

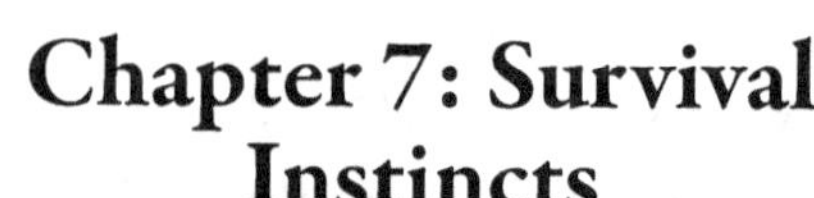

# Chapter 7: Survival Instincts

The group, having traversed the celestial anomalies and astral gateways, found themselves on the precipice of a cosmic nexus—a convergence of energies that pulsed with the intertwined destinies of the town and the cosmos. Symbols adorned the astral expanse, resonating with the choices made and the trials faced in their cosmic journey. As they approached the cosmic nexus, a sense of anticipation filled the astral currents. The guardian's echo, now a guiding force in their cosmic ties, whispered of survival instincts embedded in the very fabric of the interconnected destinies. In the heart of the cosmic nexus, the group encountered celestial reflections of their earthly selves—a manifestation of their survival instincts personified by ethereal avatars. Each avatar embodied a facet of survival—unity, adaptability, resourcefulness, and resilience. The avatars, luminous and enigmatic, beckoned the group to commune with the cosmic forces that governed their survival instincts. Symbols of survival pulsed in the astral currents, guiding the group to embrace the innate wisdom that resonated within the interconnected destinies. The avatar of unity spoke first, its cosmic echoes reverberating through the celestial nexus. "Survival is rooted in unity—a harmonious dance of cosmic forces working together. Embrace the ties that bind you, for unity is the strength that sustains the town and the cosmic realms."

With the guidance of the avatar of unity, the group delved into the cosmic currents, attuning their cosmic ties to the essence of harmonious collaboration. Symbols of unity illuminated the astral expanse, emphasizing the importance of collective strength in the face of cosmic challenges. Next, the avatar of adaptability stepped forward, its ethereal presence radiating a sense of fluidity and resilience. "Survival instincts require adaptability—a willingness to flow with the cosmic currents. Embrace change and transformation, for adaptability is the key to navigating the intricate dance of destinies."

The group, guided by the avatar of adaptability, embraced the cosmic energies that flowed through the astral expanse. Symbols of fluidity and transformation shimmered, revealing the interconnected destinies' capacity to evolve and adapt to the cosmic forces at play. The avatar of resourcefulness followed, its cosmic echoes carrying the essence of ingenuity and resourceful thinking. "Survival thrives on resourcefulness—an ability to navigate the cosmic challenges with wisdom and innovation. Embrace the cosmic knowledge within, for resourcefulness is the foundation of resilience."

With the guidance of the avatar of resourcefulness, the group tapped into the celestial wisdom embedded in the interconnected destinies. Symbols of ingenuity and cosmic knowledge manifested, highlighting the importance of leveraging cosmic insights in their ongoing journey. Finally, the avatar of resilience emerged, its luminous presence embodying the strength to endure cosmic trials. "Survival instincts demand resilience—a fortitude to face challenges with unwavering determination. Embrace the cosmic threads of resilience, for it is the backbone of survival in the grand design of destinies."

Guided by the avatar of resilience, the group strengthened their resolve, drawing upon the cosmic currents that epitomized endurance and fortitude. Symbols of resilience pulsed in the astral expanse, emphasizing the interconnected destinies' capacity to withstand the trials woven into the cosmic tapestry. As the avatars of survival instincts faded into cosmic echoes, the group stood in the cosmic nexus, their cosmic ties resonating with the essence of unity, adaptability, resourcefulness, and resilience. Symbols of survival intertwined with the threads of fate, revealing the interconnected destinies' capacity to navigate the cosmic dance with a profound understanding of the survival instincts woven into the town and the boundless cosmos. The guardian's echo, now a harmonious cadence in the astral currents, encouraged the group to carry the wisdom of survival instincts into the uncharted territories of the cosmic tapestry. Symbols of interconnected destinies illuminated their path, guiding them toward the cosmic revelations and challenges that awaited in the ongoing journey. And so, as they stepped away from the cosmic nexus, the group embraced the survival instincts embedded in their cosmic ties. The guardian's guidance echoed in their collective consciousness, urging them to navigate the interconnected destinies with a harmonious balance of unity, adaptability, resourcefulness, and resilience. The cosmic currents pulsed with a renewed vigor as the group prepared to venture further into the astral expanse. The mysteries of the interconnected destinies and the survival instincts that guided them beckoned them into the unknown—an exploration that transcended the ordinary boundaries of understanding and delved into the profound depths of the cosmic tapestry. As the group ventured deeper into the astral expanse, symbols of survival instincts continued to illuminate their path. The cosmic currents guided them toward celestial landscapes where the interconnected destinies intertwined with the essence of unity, adaptability, resourcefulness, and resilience. In the first cosmic landscape, the group encountered ethereal manifestations of unity—a collective consciousness that resonated with harmonious collaboration. Celestial symbols depicting unity pulsed with radiant light, emphasizing the strength that came from working together in the face of cosmic challenges. As they traversed the landscape of unity, the group faced astral trials that tested their ability to collaborate and unite their cosmic ties. Symbols of collaboration and collective strength guided them through celestial puzzles and challenges, highlighting the interconnected destinies' capacity to thrive when bound by the ties that united them.

Next, the group entered a cosmic realm where adaptability was the focal point. Celestial entities, embodiments of adaptability, drifted through an astral dance that mirrored the ebb and flow of cosmic energies. Symbols of fluidity and transformation shimmered, urging the group to embrace change with grace and resilience. In this celestial realm, the group encountered astral gateways that led to alternate realities shaped by adaptability. Visions unfolded, showcasing the interconnected destinies navigating cosmic shifts and transformations. The group, attuned to the cosmic currents, learned to navigate the astral gateways with a fluidity that mirrored the adaptability embedded in their cosmic ties. Continuing their astral journey, the group entered a celestial observatory where the wisdom of resourcefulness unfolded. Cosmic tomes whispered secrets of innovative thinking, and symbols of resourcefulness adorned the astral surroundings. The group communed with celestial guardians, entities of cosmic knowledge, absorbing insights that emphasized the importance of leveraging cosmic wisdom in their survival. As they explored the observatory, the group encountered celestial anomalies that challenged their resourceful thinking. Symbols of ingenuity guided them through astral riddles and puzzles, revealing the interconnected destinies' ability to navigate challenges with innovative solutions born from the cosmic knowledge that permeated the astral realms. In the final cosmic landscape, the group faced a celestial arena that embodied resilience. Ethereal manifestations of fortitude and endurance danced amidst symbols of cosmic resilience. The group, guided by the essence of resilience within their cosmic ties, engaged in celestial challenges that tested their strength and determination. As they navigated the cosmic arena, the group encountered trials that demanded unwavering resilience in the face of adversity. Symbols of endurance pulsed with cosmic light, underscoring the interconnected destinies' capacity to withstand cosmic trials and emerge stronger from the challenges woven into the fabric of the cosmic tapestry. With each celestial landscape explored, the group's survival instincts became more deeply ingrained in their cosmic ties. The guardian's echo, resonating in the astral currents, acknowledged their growth and understanding of the interconnected destinies.

As the group prepared to move forward, symbols of survival instincts continued to guide them through the astral expanse. The cosmic tapestry unfolded before them, revealing the mysteries and challenges that lay ahead. The guardian's presence, though unseen, accompanied them as a guiding force in the ongoing journey. And so, with survival instincts illuminated by celestial symbols, the group pressed on into the uncharted territories of the cosmic tapestry. The interconnected destinies and the profound wisdom of unity, adaptability, resourcefulness, and resilience propelled them further into the mysteries that awaited in the intricate dance of destinies within the boundless cosmos. As the group continued their astral journey, the cosmic tapestry unfolded before them in ever-shifting patterns of celestial energies and symbols. The survival instincts embedded in their cosmic ties guided them through astral gateways, celestial landscapes, and cosmic challenges that tested their unity, adaptability, resourcefulness, and resilience.

In the astral gateways, the group encountered glimpses of potential futures influenced by their survival instincts. Celestial symbols illuminated paths shaped by harmonious collaboration, fluid adaptation to change, innovative thinking, and unwavering resilience. The interconnected destinies of the town and the cosmos pulsed with the echoes of their choices within the astral realms. As they traversed celestial landscapes, the group witnessed the intertwined destinies navigating the cosmic dance with a profound understanding of survival instincts. Ethereal manifestations of unity, adaptability, resourcefulness, and resilience appeared, guiding them toward deeper insights into the interconnected fates that shaped the town and the boundless cosmos. In one celestial landscape, the group found themselves in a cosmic council—a gathering of celestial beings who embodied the essence of survival instincts. The celestial council, luminous and wise, spoke in cosmic echoes, imparting further wisdom on the importance of balancing their survival instincts within the intricate dance of destinies.

"The threads of fate are woven with the fabric of survival instincts," intoned a celestial being. "Harmony, adaptability, resourcefulness, and resilience are the cosmic keys that unlock the mysteries of the interconnected destinies. Embrace these instincts, for they are the guiding forces that navigate the cosmic currents."

Guided by the celestial council, the group faced astral trials that required a harmonious blend of their survival instincts. Symbols representing unity, adaptability, resourcefulness, and resilience manifested in the celestial challenges, urging the group to navigate the trials with a balance that echoed the interconnected destinies' ability to overcome cosmic obstacles. As they emerged from the cosmic council's realm, the group found themselves in a celestial observatory—a place where the cosmic knowledge of survival instincts reached its pinnacle. Symbols of ingenuity, transformative adaptability, and enduring resilience adorned the celestial observatory, offering the group an opportunity to delve even deeper into the cosmic wisdom embedded in their ties. Celestial tomes whispered cosmic secrets, and the group communed with the essence of survival instincts within the astral observatory. The guardian's echo, ever-present in the cosmic currents, encouraged them to absorb the knowledge and cosmic insights that would empower their journey into the unknown. In the final stage of their astral journey, the group entered a cosmic nexus of survival—a convergence of energies where the interconnected destinies and survival instincts intertwined. Symbols representing unity, adaptability, resourcefulness, and resilience shimmered in the cosmic nexus, inviting the group to embrace the culmination of their cosmic growth. Within the cosmic nexus, the group faced a celestial choice—a decision that would resonate with the survival instincts and shape the destiny of the town and the boundless cosmos. The symbols pulsed with cosmic significance, and the group, guided by the wisdom gained from their astral exploration, deliberated with a deep understanding of the interconnected destinies. As the symbols found their place within the cosmic nexus, the celestial energies responded with a harmonious resonance. The guardian's echo, now a symphony in the astral currents, acknowledged the group's mastery of survival instincts and the interconnected destinies that spanned the town and the vast expanse of the cosmos. With the cosmic choice made, the group emerged from the cosmic nexus, their survival instincts now finely attuned to the cosmic currents that guided their journey. Symbols of unity, adaptability, resourcefulness, and resilience pulsed in their cosmic ties, weaving a narrative of profound wisdom and resilience that transcended the ordinary boundaries of mortal understanding.

The guardian's echo, a beacon of cosmic guidance, urged the group to carry their enhanced survival instincts into the uncharted territories that awaited them. The interconnected destinies, now harmonized with the essence of unity, adaptability, resourcefulness, and resilience, beckoned them to explore the mysteries that lay beyond the known realms of the earthly and cosmic dimensions. And so, as the group stepped forward into the continuing astral journey, the guardian's echo resonated in the cosmic currents. The interconnected destinies, now illuminated by the profound wisdom of survival instincts, awaited further exploration in the intricate dance of destinies within the cosmic tapestry. The group, now enriched by the cosmic wisdom of survival instincts, ventured forth into the ever-expanding astral expanse. The guardian's echo resonated as a guiding force, urging them to navigate the interconnected destinies with newfound harmony, adaptability, resourcefulness, and resilience. Symbols of survival instincts pulsed with ethereal light, illuminating a path that led deeper into the mysteries of the cosmic tapestry. Celestial landscapes unfolded before them, each a canvas painted with cosmic energies and symbols that hinted at the intertwined destinies waiting to be unraveled. As the group traversed through the astral expanse, they encountered celestial anomalies that challenged their mastery of survival instincts. Symbols of unity tested their ability to collaborate harmoniously, adaptability presented trials of fluid navigation through change, resourcefulness demanded innovative solutions, and resilience pushed them to endure cosmic challenges with unwavering determination.

The interconnected destinies, now closely woven with the essence of survival instincts, responded to the group's actions within the celestial anomalies. Visions of potential futures echoed through the astral realms, revealing the profound impact their choices and mastery of survival instincts had on the town and the cosmic forces at play. In one celestial anomaly, the group faced a trial where unity was paramount. Celestial puzzles required them to synchronize their cosmic ties, each member contributing to the harmonic resonance that unfolded symbols of collaboration and collective strength. As they succeeded, visions unfolded, portraying a future where the town thrived in unity, its destiny interwoven with cosmic energies that echoed the group's collaborative mastery. In another anomaly, adaptability became the focal point. The astral challenges demanded the group to navigate through ever-shifting cosmic currents, symbolizing their capacity to embrace change and transformation. Visions of potential outcomes portrayed the town dynamically adapting to cosmic shifts, mirroring the group's adept navigation through the trials of adaptability. The cosmic anomalies continued, each highlighting the importance of resourcefulness and resilience in the face of challenges. The group's mastery of survival instincts influenced the celestial trials, shaping visions of potential futures where cosmic knowledge and unwavering fortitude played pivotal roles in the town's destiny. As the group emerged from the celestial anomalies, their cosmic ties resonated with the enriched survival instincts that guided their journey. The guardian's echo whispered words of encouragement, acknowledging the profound growth within their interconnected destinies and the impact on the grand tapestry of the cosmos. Guided by their harmonized survival instincts, the group reached a celestial convergence—a nexus where the threads of fate and the cosmic forces intermingled. Symbols representing unity, adaptability, resourcefulness, and resilience pulsed in a harmonious dance, reflecting the culmination of their astral exploration and the choices made within the interconnected destinies.

In this cosmic nexus, the group faced a cosmic revelation—a manifestation of the town's collective consciousness intertwined with the essence of survival instincts. The celestial entity, radiant with the cosmic forces, acknowledged the group's journey and the wisdom gained through their mastery of survival instincts.

"You have traversed the astral realms, faced celestial trials, and harmonized the survival instincts within your cosmic ties," intoned the celestial entity. "The interconnected destinies respond to your choices and resonate with the essence of unity, adaptability, resourcefulness, and resilience. As stewards of the town's destiny, continue to explore the cosmic tapestry with reverence and wisdom."

With the cosmic entity's words echoing in the astral currents, the group prepared to move forward, guided by the enhanced survival instincts that now shaped their cosmic ties. Symbols of interconnected destinies illuminated the path ahead, inviting them to explore the mysteries that lay beyond the known realms of the earthly and cosmic dimensions. And so, as the group stepped into the continuing journey, the guardian's echo resonated with cosmic assurance. The interconnected destinies, now intricately bound with the profound wisdom of survival instincts, unfolded before them in the intricate dance of destinies within the vast expanse of the cosmic tapestry. The mysteries of the cosmic forces and the town's destiny beckoned, and the group, custodians of survival instincts, embraced the ongoing exploration into the unknown with a sense of purpose and cosmic reverence.

# Chapter 8: Fractured Unity

The group, guided by the harmonized survival instincts within their cosmic ties, continued their journey through the astral expanse. Symbols of interconnected destinies pulsed with ethereal light, leading them toward a celestial crossroads—a convergence point where the threads of fate and the cosmic forces intersected. As they approached the cosmic crossroads, a subtle tension lingered in the astral currents. The guardian's echo, ever present, whispered of challenges that awaited, challenging the unity forged within the group's cosmic ties. Symbols of unity, though radiant, seemed to flicker with uncertainty, hinting at the potential for discord within the interconnected destinies. The group entered a celestial realm where the fabric of unity was tested. Ethereal manifestations of conflicting energies appeared, creating a cosmic tension that resonated with the trials of the town's destiny. Symbols of fractured unity shimmered in the astral expanse, reflecting the challenges that awaited the group. Within this celestial realm, the group encountered astral gateways leading to alternate realities where unity was put to the test. Visions unfolded, portraying potential futures where the town's destiny splintered into divergent paths influenced by internal conflicts and discord among its residents. In one reality, the group witnessed a fracturing of unity as mistrust and hidden agendas eroded the cosmic bonds that once held the town together. Symbols of discord pulsed through the astral landscapes, revealing the consequences of internal strife within the interconnected destinies. In another reality, the group glimpsed a future where external threats exploited the vulnerabilities caused by a lack of unity. Celestial forces of chaos and dissonance wreaked havoc upon the town, emphasizing the importance of cohesive collaboration in the face of cosmic challenges.

The guardian's echo resonated with a sense of caution, guiding the group to navigate the celestial anomalies with a heightened awareness of the potential fractures within the interconnected destinies. Symbols of unity flickered, responding to the group's choices as they faced trials designed to test the strength of their harmonized survival instincts. As the group moved through the celestial anomalies, they encountered astral puzzles and challenges that demanded unity and collaboration. The symbols of fractured unity, though persistent, responded positively to the group's efforts to overcome discord and reinforce the cosmic ties that bound them together. In the heart of the celestial realm, the group faced a cosmic choice—a decision that would either mend the fractures within the town's destiny or deepen the rifts that threatened to tear it apart. Symbols of unity and discord shimmered in the astral currents, reflecting the delicate balance between harmonious collaboration and internal strife. With the cosmic choice made, the group emerged from the celestial realm, their cosmic ties now marked by the echoes of the challenges they faced. The guardian's guidance, though tempered, acknowledged the group's resilience in the face of fractured unity and the potential for discord within the interconnected destinies. The astral expanse unfolded before them, revealing a path that continued to explore the consequences of internal conflicts and the challenges of navigating the cosmic tapestry with fractured unity. Symbols of interconnected destinies pulsed, inviting the group to delve deeper into the mysteries that lay ahead in the intricate dance of destinies within the vast expanse of the cosmic tapestry.

As the group ventured further into the astral expanse, the echoes of fractured unity lingered in the cosmic currents. Symbols of interconnected destinies pulsed with a subtle tension, reflecting the challenges posed by internal discord within the town's destiny. The celestial landscapes unfolded, revealing alternate realities where the consequences of fractured unity manifested in different ways. In one astral realm, the group witnessed a town divided along ideological lines, with conflicting factions vying for dominance. Symbols of discord and polarization shimmered in the astral expanse, portraying a future shaped by internal strife. In another reality, the group glimpsed a town weakened by distrust and suspicion, its residents isolated and fragmented. Celestial energies of dissonance permeated the astral landscapes, underscoring the impact of fractured unity on the interconnected destinies. Guided by the guardian's echo, the group encountered celestial beings—ethereal entities that personified the consequences of internal discord. These cosmic beings, manifestations of the fractured unity within the town, spoke in cosmic echoes, urging the group to confront the underlying tensions that threatened to unravel the fabric of the interconnected destinies.

"The threads of fate are delicate and easily frayed by internal conflicts," intoned one cosmic being. "Harmony within the interconnected destinies is the key to navigating the cosmic currents. Seek the root causes of discord and strive for a unity that transcends the challenges that threaten to tear you apart.

"As the group navigated through the astral realms, they faced trials designed to address the fractures within their cosmic ties. Celestial puzzles challenged their ability to communicate and collaborate effectively, and symbols of unity responded dynamically to their choices, flickering with the potential for resolution or further discord.

In the heart of a celestial convergence, the group encountered a cosmic anomaly—a manifestation of the town's collective consciousness grappling with the consequences of fractured unity. Symbols of discord and unity interwove in a cosmic dance, creating a dynamic tapestry that reflected the group's choices and their impact on the town's destiny. The guardian's echo guided the group to a pivotal moment within the celestial anomaly—a moment where the cosmic forces responded to their decisions. Symbols representing the group's efforts to mend the fractures within the interconnected destinies pulsed with ethereal light, signaling a potential resolution to the challenges of internal discord. With each collaborative choice made by the group, the symbols of unity grew stronger, harmonizing with the cosmic currents that shaped the town's destiny. The celestial anomaly, once fraught with tension, transformed into a tableau of interconnected destinies mending the fractures within their cosmic ties. As the group emerged from the celestial anomaly, the guardian's echo resonated with a sense of accomplishment. The symbols of interconnected destinies now glowed with a renewed vibrancy, reflecting the group's commitment to fostering unity amidst the challenges of the cosmic tapestry. The astral expanse stretched out before them, inviting the group to continue their exploration of the interconnected destinies. Symbols of unity, though still flickering, pulsed with a newfound strength, echoing the group's resilience in the face of internal discord. And so, with the echoes of fractured unity behind them, the group pressed on into the cosmic tapestry, guided by the harmonized survival instincts that now bore the imprints of their efforts to mend the town's destiny. The mysteries of the interconnected destinies awaited further unraveling, and the guardian's echo urged the group to embrace the ongoing journey with a profound understanding of the delicate balance between unity and discord within the vast expanse of the cosmic tapestry.

# Chapter 9: Revelations in the Dark

The group, having navigated the challenges of fractured unity within the astral realms, now found themselves drawn toward a cosmic convergence shrouded in shadows—a celestial realm veiled in mystery and revelation. Symbols of interconnected destinies glowed dimly in the dark, hinting at profound cosmic secrets waiting to be unveiled. As they ventured deeper into the astral expanse, the guardian's echo spoke of a cosmic threshold where revelations in the dark would test the group's resilience and illuminate the obscured truths woven into the fabric of the interconnected destinies. The celestial landscapes shifted into a surreal, dimly lit realm where shadows danced with cosmic energies. Symbols of revelation adorned the astral expanse, beckoning the group to explore the obscured truths that lay hidden within the intricate dance of destinies. In this cosmic twilight, the group encountered ethereal manifestations of forgotten memories and untold secrets. Symbols of revelation pulsed with a subtle luminosity, guiding them toward astral gateways that led to fragments of the interconnected destinies obscured by the shadows of time. As the group traversed through the celestial gateways, visions unfolded—glimpses into the past, present, and potential futures influenced by the revelations in the dark. Cosmic echoes whispered forgotten tales, and symbols of interconnected destinies shimmered with the latent energies of untold cosmic secrets.

In one fragment of revelation, the group witnessed a forgotten chapter from the town's history—a moment obscured by the shadows of time. Symbols of interconnected destinies depicted a narrative of lost connections, buried truths, and the impact of untold stories on the town's destiny. In another revelation, the group glimpsed a cosmic convergence where the threads of fate intertwined with celestial forces beyond mortal comprehension. Symbols of revelation illuminated the astral expanse, revealing a cosmic tapestry interwoven with the destinies of beings beyond the earthly realm. Guided by the guardian's echo, the group faced celestial challenges within the darkened realms—trials that tested their ability to unveil obscured truths and face the cosmic revelations with open hearts. Symbols of revelation responded dynamically to their choices, reflecting the profound impact of their decisions on the interconnected destinies. As they explored further, the group encountered celestial entities—guardians of the obscured truths—entities that spoke in cosmic echoes, offering guidance on how to navigate the revelations in the dark.

"Within the shadows lie the forgotten tales and cosmic mysteries that shape the destinies of the town and the boundless cosmos," intoned a celestial entity. "Embrace the revelations in the dark with a keen eye, for within the obscured truths lies the wisdom that transcends the ordinary boundaries of understanding."

The group, attuned to the cosmic energies, delved into the mysteries that unfolded within the darkened realms. Symbols of revelation guided them toward celestial anomalies—pockets of energy where untold secrets awaited discovery. In one anomaly, the group faced trials that required them to unveil obscured memories—a cosmic puzzle where symbols of interconnected destinies intertwined with forgotten tales. As they succeeded, visions of the town's history, once veiled in shadows, emerged with a newfound clarity. In another anomaly, the group encountered celestial reflections of potential futures shaped by the revelations in the dark. Symbols of interconnected destinies pulsed with cosmic energies, offering glimpses into the threads of fate influenced by the untold secrets that lay hidden within the cosmic tapestry. With each revelation, the group's understanding of the interconnected destinies deepened. The guardian's echo, a steady guide in the astral currents, encouraged them to embrace the cosmic mysteries with a sense of reverence and curiosity. As the group continued their exploration, symbols of revelation continued to illuminate the darkened realms. The cosmic tapestry unfolded before them, revealing the intertwined destinies shaped by the untold secrets and forgotten tales hidden within the shadows of time. With revelations in the dark guiding their path, the group pressed on into the cosmic tapestry, ready to unveil the obscured truths that held the key to the town's destiny and the boundless mysteries that awaited in the intricate dance of destinies within the vast expanse of the astral realms.

The group, now enveloped in the cosmic twilight of revelations in the dark, pressed forward into the heart of the astral expanse. Symbols of interconnected destinies pulsed with a subtle luminosity, guiding them toward celestial anomalies where cosmic secrets waited to be unveiled. In one celestial anomaly, the group encountered a cosmic mirror—a manifestation of the interconnected destinies reflecting untold truths and obscured memories. Symbols of revelation shimmered as the mirror unveiled forgotten tales and cosmic echoes that resonated with the group's journey through time. As the group gazed into the cosmic mirror, visions of pivotal moments from the town's history unfolded. Forgotten faces, echoes of long-lost conversations, and the repercussions of decisions made in the shadows of the past emerged with ethereal clarity. Symbols of interconnected destinies resonated with the cosmic energies, underscoring the impact of these revelations on the fabric of the town's destiny. In another anomaly, the group faced a celestial riddle—a puzzle woven with symbols of revelation and obscured cosmic truths. Guided by the guardian's echo, they deciphered the enigmatic patterns within the astral currents, unraveling the mysteries hidden within the cosmic tapestry. With each revelation, the group's cosmic ties resonated with a deeper understanding of the interconnected destinies. The guardian's presence, though unseen, echoed words of encouragement, urging them to continue their quest for cosmic wisdom within the shadows of time. The group entered a cosmic archive—a repository of untold stories and forgotten knowledge. Celestial tomes whispered cosmic secrets, and symbols of revelation adorned the astral surroundings. Guided by the guardian's echo, they delved into the cosmic knowledge within the archive, absorbing insights that transcended the ordinary boundaries of mortal understanding. In the heart of the cosmic archive, the group faced a celestial conundrum—a choice that would either deepen the mysteries shrouded in the dark or unveil a cosmic revelation that held the potential to shape the destinies of the town and the boundless cosmos. Symbols of revelation pulsed with anticipation as the group deliberated on the cosmic choice before them. The guardian's echo, a reassuring presence in the astral currents, encouraged them to trust in the interconnected destinies and embrace the revelations in the dark with a sense of cosmic reverence. With the cosmic choice made, the group witnessed a surge of cosmic energy within the archive. Symbols of interconnected destinies responded to their decision, unraveling further secrets and unveiling untold cosmic truths that rippled through the fabric of the astral expanse. As they emerged from the cosmic archive, the group's cosmic ties resonated with the newfound revelations in the dark. Symbols of interconnected destinies pulsed with a radiant luminosity, echoing the group's success in unveiling cosmic truths and forging a deeper connection with the boundless mysteries of the astral realms. The guardian's echo, now a harmonious cadence in the astral currents, congratulated the group on their journey through revelations in the dark. Symbols of cosmic wisdom adorned their cosmic ties, guiding them toward the next phase of their exploration within the intricate dance of destinies. With the echoes of revelations in the dark guiding their path, the group continued into the cosmic tapestry, ready to face the mysteries that lay beyond the shadows of time. Symbols of interconnected destinies illuminated their way, beckoning them to explore the profound depths of the astral realms and uncover the cosmic truths that awaited in the ongoing journey within the vast expanse of the cosmic tapestry.

As the group ventured deeper into the astral expanse, guided by the revelations in the dark, symbols of interconnected destinies continued to pulse with a radiant luminosity. The cosmic tapestry unfolded before them, revealing celestial landscapes that held the echoes of cosmic truths and untold stories. In the heart of a celestial convergence, the group encountered a cosmic portal—a gateway that led to a realm where the threads of fate intertwined with the cosmic forces of revelation. Symbols of interconnected destinies shimmered around the portal, inviting the group to step through and explore the revelations that awaited on the other side. As they traversed the cosmic portal, the group found themselves in a realm where time and space intertwined in a surreal dance. Celestial energies of revelation danced through the astral currents, weaving a tapestry of cosmic truths that transcended the ordinary boundaries of mortal understanding. In this ethereal realm, the group encountered celestial beings—guardians of the cosmic revelations. These entities, luminous and wise, spoke in harmonious echoes, sharing insights that resonated with the group's journey through the shadows of time.

"The revelations in the dark hold the key to understanding the interconnected destinies and the cosmic forces that shape the town's destiny," intoned a celestial being. "Embrace the cosmic truths that unfold before you, for they carry the wisdom of the astral realms and the boundless mysteries that await in the intricate dance of destinies."

Guided by the celestial guardians, the group faced celestial challenges within this surreal realm—trials that required them to attune their cosmic ties to the revelations in the dark. Symbols of interconnected destinies responded dynamically to their choices, reflecting the profound impact of their decisions on the unfolding cosmic narrative. In one celestial challenge, the group encountered a cosmic enigma—a puzzle where symbols of revelation and interconnected destinies interwove in intricate patterns. Guided by the guardian's echo, they deciphered the astral symbols, unraveling the cosmic mysteries hidden within the celestial enigma. As they progressed through the surreal realm, the group faced manifestations of cosmic forces influenced by the revelations in the dark. Symbols of interconnected destinies pulsed with cosmic energies, revealing potential futures shaped by the wisdom gained from their journey through the shadows of time. In the heart of the celestial convergence, the group confronted a cosmic choice—a decision that would either deepen their understanding of the interconnected destinies or obscure the cosmic truths in veils of uncertainty. Symbols of revelation and destiny shimmered with anticipation, inviting the group to make a choice that resonated with the essence of the revelations in the dark. With the cosmic choice made, the group felt a surge of cosmic energy. Symbols of interconnected destinies responded to their decision, aligning with the unfolding revelations and imbuing their cosmic ties with a profound luminosity. As they emerged from the surreal realm, the guardian's echo resonated with a sense of cosmic fulfillment. Symbols of revelation and interconnected destinies glowed brightly in the astral currents, reflecting the group's success in navigating the cosmic forces that shaped the town's destiny. The celestial convergence expanded into a cosmic tapestry that stretched before them, inviting the group to continue their exploration within the vast expanse of the astral realms. Symbols of interconnected destinies illuminated the path ahead, urging them to delve deeper into the mysteries that lay beyond the known realms of the earthly and cosmic dimensions.

The group, now surrounded by the radiant glow of cosmic truths unveiled in the surreal realm, continued their journey through the astral expanse. Symbols of interconnected destinies pulsed with newfound luminosity, casting ethereal light on the cosmic tapestry that unfolded before them. As they traversed through the astral landscapes, the guardian's echo resonated with a sense of cosmic satisfaction, acknowledging the group's profound exploration of revelations in the dark. The symbols of interconnected destinies, now infused with the wisdom gained from the surreal realm, guided them toward the next phase of their cosmic journey. In the heart of a celestial nexus, the group encountered an astral gateway leading to the cosmic echoes—a realm where the threads of fate reverberated with the accumulated cosmic knowledge of the interconnected destinies. Symbols of revelation adorned the astral gateway, inviting the group to step through and commune with the echoes of cosmic wisdom. As they entered the realm of cosmic echoes, the group found themselves surrounded by ethereal manifestations of the interconnected destinies. Symbols of revelation shimmered in the astral currents, echoing the untold stories, forgotten tales, and cosmic truths that resonated within the threads of fate. Celestial echoes spoke in harmonious cadence, recounting the history of the town, the cosmic forces at play, and the intricate dance of destinies within the vast expanse of the astral realms. The group, attuned to the cosmic energies, absorbed the echoes of cosmic wisdom, deepening their understanding of the interconnected destinies. In one cosmic echo, the group witnessed pivotal moments where the town's destiny intersected with celestial forces. Symbols of revelation illuminated the astral surroundings, offering insights into the cosmic currents that shaped the destinies of the town and its residents. In another echo, the group delved into the collective consciousness of the town—an astral realm where the thoughts, emotions, and aspirations of its residents echoed through the cosmic tapestry. Symbols of interconnected destinies pulsed with the harmonies and discordances within the collective consciousness, revealing the profound impact of individual choices on the town's destiny. Guided by the guardian's echo, the group faced celestial challenges within the realm of cosmic echoes—trials that required them to navigate the intricate dance of destinies within the astral currents. Symbols of revelation and interconnected destinies responded dynamically to their choices, reflecting the resonance of their decisions within the cosmic echoes. As they progressed through the realm of cosmic echoes, the group encountered celestial entities—guardians of the threads of fate. These luminous beings, embodiments of cosmic knowledge, spoke in echoes that reverberated through the astral currents, imparting wisdom that transcended mortal understanding.

"The interconnected destinies are woven into the fabric of the cosmic tapestry," intoned a celestial entity. "Within the echoes of cosmic wisdom, discover the threads that bind the destinies of the town and the boundless cosmos. Embrace the harmonies and discordances, for they hold the key to navigating the intricate dance of destinies."

With the guardian's guidance, the group faced a cosmic convergence within the realm of cosmic echoes—a moment where the threads of fate converged with the group's choices. Symbols of interconnected destinies pulsed with cosmic energy, inviting the group to make a choice that would resonate with the essence of the cosmic echoes. As the group made their cosmic choice, the realm of cosmic echoes responded with a harmonious resonance. Symbols of revelation and interconnected destinies aligned, creating a luminous tableau that reflected the group's mastery of the cosmic forces that shaped the town's destiny. With the cosmic echoes resonating in the astral currents, the guardian's echo spoke with a profound sense of fulfillment. Symbols of interconnected destinies, now imbued with the wisdom gained from the realm of cosmic echoes, guided the group toward the next phase of their exploration within the boundless cosmos. The astral gateway beckoned, leading the group toward uncharted territories where the mysteries of the cosmic tapestry awaited further unraveling. Symbols of revelation and interconnected destinies illuminated their path, inviting them to delve deeper into the astral realms and uncover the cosmic truths that lay beyond the known realms of the earthly and cosmic dimensions. And so, with the echoes of cosmic wisdom guiding their way, the group pressed on into the continuing cosmic tapestry. The interconnected destinies, now enriched by the revelations in the dark and the resonance of cosmic echoes, awaited further exploration in the intricate dance of destinies within the vast expanse of the astral realms.

The group, having absorbed the cosmic wisdom from the realm of cosmic echoes, moved forward into the unexplored reaches of the astral expanse. Symbols of interconnected destinies pulsed with a luminous brilliance, guiding them toward celestial anomalies where the threads of fate continued to weave a tapestry of cosmic truths. As they traversed through the astral landscapes, the guardian's echo whispered words of encouragement, acknowledging the group's mastery of the cosmic forces that shaped the town's destiny. Symbols of revelation continued to illuminate their path, urging them to uncover the mysteries that awaited in the ongoing journey within the vast expanse of the cosmic tapestry. In one celestial anomaly, the group encountered a cosmic convergence of forgotten memories—a place where symbols of revelation interwove with ethereal manifestations of untold stories. Guided by the guardian's echo, they delved into the astral currents, unraveling the cosmic mysteries hidden within the fragmented memories of the interconnected destinies. As the group explored further, they faced trials that tested their ability to navigate the complexities of the cosmic tapestry. Celestial puzzles challenged their understanding of interconnected destinies, urging them to seek harmony within the threads of fate and unveil the cosmic truths that shaped the town's destiny. In the heart of a celestial convergence, the group confronted a manifestation of cosmic choices—a moment where symbols of revelation and interconnected destinies pulsed with cosmic energy. The guardian's echo guided them to make choices that resonated with the essence of the ongoing journey, deepening their understanding of the intricate dance of destinies.

With each choice made, the symbols of interconnected destinies responded dynamically, revealing potential futures influenced by the group's decisions. The guardian's echo, a steady presence in the astral currents, spoke of the importance of their choices in shaping the destinies of the town and the cosmic forces that bound the threads of fate. In the cosmic tapestry that unfolded before them, the group encountered celestial entities—guardians of cosmic revelations. These luminous beings, embodiments of the cosmic forces, spoke in harmonious echoes, sharing insights that transcended mortal understanding.

"The threads of fate are intertwined with the cosmic forces that shape the destinies of the town and the boundless cosmos," intoned a celestial entity. "Continue to embrace the revelations in the dark and the echoes of cosmic wisdom, for within them lies the key to navigating the ongoing journey within the astral realms."

As the group moved through the celestial anomalies, symbols of revelation and interconnected destinies continued to guide their path. The guardian's echo, resonating with cosmic assurance, urged them to explore the mysteries that lay beyond the known realms of the earthly and cosmic dimensions. And so, with the echoes of cosmic wisdom and revelations in the dark guiding their way, the group pressed on into the continuing cosmic tapestry. The interconnected destinies, now enriched by the resonance of cosmic forces, awaited further exploration in the intricate dance of destinies within the vast expanse of the astral realms.

The group, now deeply attuned to the cosmic forces and guided by the echoes of cosmic wisdom, ventured into a celestial convergence where the threads of fate intertwined with the ever-expanding tapestry of interconnected destinies. Symbols of revelation and cosmic energies pulsed in harmony, revealing potential futures shaped by the choices made within the astral realms. In this cosmic convergence, the group faced a manifestation of the town's collective consciousness—a surreal realm where symbols of revelation and interconnected destinies danced in ethereal patterns. The guardian's echo, a steady presence in the astral currents, urged the group to navigate the complexities of this cosmic tapestry with a profound understanding of the interconnected destinies. As they moved through the celestial convergence, the group encountered celestial anomalies that reflected the consequences of their choices within the interconnected destinies. Symbols of revelation responded dynamically to their decisions, illuminating potential futures influenced by the group's mastery of the cosmic forces. In one anomaly, the group glimpsed a vision of the town thriving in harmony—a future where the threads of fate interwove with cosmic energies, and symbols of revelation portrayed a tapestry shaped by collaborative efforts and enlightened choices. In another anomaly, the group faced the echoes of discord—a potential future where internal conflicts and disharmony marred the town's destiny. Symbols of revelation shimmered in dissonant patterns, underscoring the importance of navigating the intricacies of the interconnected destinies with wisdom and unity. Guided by the guardian's echo, the group encountered cosmic beings—entities that embodied the essence of revelation and interconnected destinies. These luminous entities spoke in harmonious echoes, offering insights into the ongoing journey within the astral realms.

"WITHIN THE COSMIC TAPESTRY, the threads of fate respond to your choices and the mastery of cosmic forces," intoned a celestial being. "Continue to seek revelations in the dark, for they hold the key to unlocking the true potential of the interconnected destinies."

As the group navigated through the celestial anomalies, symbols of revelation and interconnected destinies continued to guide their path. The guardian's echo, now an ever-present guide in the astral currents, encouraged them to explore the mysteries that lay beyond the known realms of the earthly and cosmic dimensions. In the heart of a cosmic nexus, the group faced a pivotal moment—a manifestation of choices that resonated through the interconnected destinies. Symbols of revelation and cosmic energies pulsed with anticipation, inviting the group to make decisions that would shape the ongoing narrative within the cosmic tapestry. With each choice made, the cosmic energies responded dynamically, shaping the astral currents and weaving new patterns within the interconnected destinies. The guardian's echo, a soothing presence in the cosmic currents, acknowledged the group's profound influence on the town's destiny and the boundless cosmos. As the group emerged from the cosmic nexus, symbols of revelation and interconnected destinies continued to glow with a radiant luminosity. The astral expanse stretched out before them, inviting further exploration of the mysteries that awaited in the ongoing journey within the vast expanse of the cosmic tapestry. With the echoes of cosmic wisdom guiding their way, the group pressed on into the continuing cosmic tapestry. The interconnected destinies, now enriched by the mastery of cosmic forces, awaited further unraveling in the intricate dance of destinies within the astral realms.

As the group continued their journey through the astral expanse, symbols of revelation and interconnected destinies guided them toward a celestial convergence where the fabric of the cosmic tapestry seemed to ripple with potentialities. The guardian's echo, a harmonious presence in the astral currents, spoke of the significance of the choices made within the interconnected destinies. In this celestial convergence, the group encountered a cosmic crossroads—a nexus where the threads of fate intersected with the cosmic forces. Symbols of revelation and interconnected destinies pulsed with cosmic energies, inviting the group to make choices that would shape the ongoing narrative within the intricate dance of destinies. As they navigated through the cosmic crossroads, the group faced ethereal manifestations of potential futures. Symbols of revelation illuminated the astral surroundings, portraying a myriad of destinies influenced by the group's decisions. The guardian's echo, resonating with cosmic assurance, encouraged them to embrace the gravity of their choices within the vast expanse of the interconnected destinies. In one manifestation, the group glimpsed a future where the town's destiny flourished—a tapestry woven with collaborative efforts, enlightened decisions, and harmonious energies. Symbols of revelation shimmered in vibrant patterns, reflecting the potential for prosperity and unity within the interconnected destinies. In another manifestation, the group witnessed the consequences of discord—a potential future where internal conflicts and disharmony cast shadows upon the town's destiny. Symbols of revelation flickered with dissonant energies, underscoring the delicate balance between unity and discord within the cosmic tapestry.

Guided by the guardian's echo, the group encountered celestial entities—watchers of the cosmic crossroads. These luminous beings, embodiments of revelation and interconnected destinies, spoke in echoes that reverberated through the astral currents, offering guidance on navigating the intricacies of the ongoing journey.

"The choices you make within the cosmic crossroads ripple through the interconnected destinies," intoned a celestial entity. "Seek revelations in the dark, for they hold the key to unlocking the true potential of the threads of fate. The cosmic tapestry is woven with the threads of your decisions, and within them lies the essence of the town's destiny."

As the group faced celestial challenges within the cosmic crossroads, symbols of revelation and interconnected destinies responded dynamically to their choices. The astral currents pulsed with cosmic energies, reflecting the impact of their decisions on the fabric of the cosmic tapestry. In the heart of the celestial convergence, the group confronted a cosmic choice—a decision that would echo through the interconnected destinies and shape the ongoing narrative within the vast expanse of the astral realms. Symbols of revelation and cosmic energies glowed with anticipation, inviting the group to make a choice that resonated with the essence of their journey. With the cosmic choice made, the guardian's echo resonated with a sense of cosmic fulfillment. Symbols of revelation and interconnected destinies aligned, creating a luminous tableau that reflected the group's influence on the town's destiny and the boundless cosmos. As they emerged from the cosmic crossroads, the guardian's echo urged the group to continue their exploration within the astral realms. Symbols of revelation and interconnected destinies illuminated their path, inviting them to delve deeper into the mysteries that lay beyond the known realms of the earthly and cosmic dimensions. And so, with the echoes of cosmic wisdom and revelations in the dark guiding their way, the group pressed on into the continuing cosmic tapestry. The interconnected destinies, now enriched by the choices made within the cosmic crossroads, awaited further exploration in the intricate dance of destinies within the vast expanse of the astral realms.

# Chapter 10: The Point of No Return

As the group ventured deeper into the astral realms, the luminous symbols of interconnected destinies guided them toward a cosmic nexus known as the Point of No Return. In this celestial convergence, the threads of fate converged with cosmic forces, creating a pivotal moment that would shape the town's destiny and the intricate dance of destinies within the vast expanse of the astral realms. The guardian's echo, a steadfast presence in the astral currents, spoke of the significance of the Point of No Return—a cosmic threshold where the choices made would ripple through the fabric of the interconnected destinies, leading the group toward the culmination of their journey. Symbols of revelation pulsed with cosmic energy as the group approached the Point of No Return. The astral expanse stretched out before them, inviting them to confront the mysteries that awaited within this pivotal convergence of cosmic forces.

In the heart of the celestial nexus, the group encountered ethereal manifestations of potential futures. Symbols of revelation shimmered in intricate patterns, portraying the consequences of their choices and the impact on the town's destiny. The guardian's echo encouraged them to approach the cosmic threshold with a deep understanding of the interconnected destinies and the boundless cosmos. As the group navigated through the celestial anomalies within the Point of No Return, they faced trials that tested their resolve and wisdom. Celestial puzzles, cosmic challenges, and manifestations of revelation awaited, urging them to demonstrate mastery over the cosmic forces that governed the threads of fate. In one cosmic anomaly, the group encountered a reflection of the town's destiny shaped by their journey through revelations in the dark, cosmic echoes, and the cosmic crossroads. Symbols of interconnected destinies responded dynamically to their choices, creating a living tapestry that reflected the culmination of their efforts within the astral realms. In another anomaly, the group faced a celestial enigma—a puzzle woven with symbols of revelation and cosmic energies. Guided by the guardian's echo, they deciphered the intricate patterns within the astral currents, unraveling the mysteries hidden within the fabric of the Point of No Return. As the group progressed through the celestial challenges, the guardian's echo spoke of the cosmic choices that lay ahead—choices that would either solidify the town's destiny in harmonious unity or push it to the brink of discord. Symbols of revelation and interconnected destinies pulsed with anticipation, reflecting the gravity of the impending decisions within the astral realms.

In the heart of the Point of No Return, the group confronted a cosmic convergence—a moment where the threads of fate converged with their choices. Symbols of revelation and interconnected destinies glowed with a transcendent luminosity, inviting the group to make decisions that would resonate with the essence of their journey. With each choice made, the fabric of the Point of No Return responded dynamically, creating a cosmic tableau that reflected the culmination of the group's mastery over the interconnected destinies. The guardian's echo, a harmonious cadence in the astral currents, acknowledged the significance of their choices within the ongoing dance of destinies. As the group emerged from the Point of No Return, symbols of revelation and interconnected destinies continued to glow with a radiant luminosity. The astral expanse stretched out before them, inviting further exploration of the mysteries that awaited in the intricate dance of destinies within the vast expanse of the cosmic tapestry. As the group ventured forth from the Point of No Return, the luminous symbols of interconnected destinies continued to guide them through the astral realms. The guardian's echo, a constant companion in the cosmic currents, spoke of the consequences and potentialities that now unfolded within the fabric of the cosmic tapestry. Symbols of revelation pulsed with a newfound intensity, reflecting the group's journey through the celestial challenges and pivotal choices made at the Point of No Return. The astral expanse, ever-expanding and filled with cosmic energies, beckoned the group to delve even deeper into the mysteries that lay ahead. In the aftermath of the cosmic convergence, the group encountered celestial anomalies that resonated with the consequences of their choices. Symbols of interconnected destinies shimmered with ethereal light, portraying the ongoing narrative of the town's destiny and the threads of fate interwoven within the astral realms.

In one anomaly, the group witnessed echoes of unity—a potential future where the interconnected destinies flourished in harmonious balance. Symbols of revelation illuminated the astral surroundings, underscoring the impact of their choices in fostering collaboration and enlightenment within the town's destiny. In another anomaly, the group faced manifestations of discord—a potential future where the threads of fate unraveled in disharmony. Symbols of revelation flickered with dissonant energies, revealing the consequences of decisions that strained the interconnected destinies and pushed the town toward the brink of chaos. Guided by the guardian's echo, the group encountered celestial entities—watchers of the ongoing cosmic tapestry. These luminous beings, embodiments of revelation and interconnected destinies, spoke in echoes that reverberated through the astral currents, offering insights into the continuing journey.

"The Point of No Return marked a pivotal moment, but the threads of fate continue to weave," intoned a celestial entity. "Within the ongoing dance of destinies, seek further revelations in the dark, for the cosmic tapestry holds both the echoes of the past and the potentialities of the future."

As the group navigated through the celestial anomalies, symbols of revelation and interconnected destinies continued to guide their path. The guardian's echo, resonating with cosmic assurance, urged them to explore the mysteries that lay beyond the known realms of the earthly and cosmic dimensions. In the heart of a celestial nexus, the group faced a manifestation of the astral currents—a convergence of cosmic forces that echoed with the consequences of their choices. Symbols of revelation and interconnected destinies pulsed with cosmic energy, inviting the group to reflect on the ongoing narrative within the intricate dance of destinies. With each reflection, the group deepened their understanding of the interconnected destinies and the profound impact of their choices within the astral realms. The guardian's echo, a soothing presence in the cosmic currents, acknowledged their evolving mastery over the cosmic forces and encouraged them to press on into the mysteries that awaited. The group, now immersed in the ongoing cosmic tapestry, followed the radiant symbols of interconnected destinies through the astral realms. The guardian's echo remained a steadfast guide, its ethereal resonance echoing through the cosmic currents, reminding the group of the ever-evolving dance of destinies. As the group traversed through the astral expanse, they encountered celestial anomalies that reflected the repercussions of their journey. Symbols of revelation pulsed with a rhythmic luminosity, portraying potential futures influenced by the threads of fate and the choices made at the Point of No Return. In one anomaly, the group witnessed echoes of transformation—a potential future where the interconnected destinies underwent a profound metamorphosis. Symbols of revelation illuminated the astral surroundings, revealing a tapestry woven with growth, enlightenment, and the harmonious evolution of the town's destiny.

In another anomaly, the group faced manifestations of stagnation—a potential future where the threads of fate lingered in inertia. Symbols of revelation flickered with subdued energies, portraying the consequences of choices that hindered progress and veiled the interconnected destinies in a cosmic standstill. Guided by the guardian's echo, the group encountered celestial entities—custodians of the ongoing cosmic tapestry. These luminous beings, embodiments of revelation and interconnected destinies, spoke in echoes that resonated through the astral currents, offering guidance on navigating the complexities of the continuing journey.

"The cosmic tapestry is a living narrative, shaped by the choices made within the astral realms," intoned a celestial entity. "As you explore further revelations in the dark, remember that the threads of fate respond to your influence. Embrace the ongoing dance of destinies with wisdom and purpose."

As the group progressed through the celestial anomalies, symbols of revelation and interconnected destinies responded dynamically to their choices. The astral currents pulsed with cosmic energy, reflecting the group's evolving mastery over the interconnected destinies and the cosmic forces that guided the threads of fate. In the heart of a celestial nexus, the group faced a manifestation of the astral currents—a convergence of cosmic forces that echoed with the consequences of their choices. Symbols of revelation and interconnected destinies pulsed with anticipation, inviting the group to reflect on the ongoing narrative within the intricate dance of destinies. With each reflection, the group deepened their understanding of the interconnected destinies and the profound impact of their choices within the astral realms. The guardian's echo, a harmonious cadence in the cosmic currents, acknowledged their evolving mastery over the cosmic forces and encouraged them to press on into the mysteries that awaited. As they emerged from the celestial nexus, symbols of revelation and interconnected destinies continued to glow with a radiant luminosity.

The astral expanse stretched out before them, inviting further exploration of the mysteries that lay beyond the known realms of the earthly and cosmic dimensions. As the group delved deeper into the astral realms, the luminous symbols of interconnected destinies continued to guide them through the celestial anomalies. The guardian's echo, a steady presence in the cosmic currents, resonated with a deep wisdom that echoed through the ongoing dance of destinies. Symbols of revelation pulsed with a rhythmic luminosity, portraying the evolving narrative of the town's destiny. The astral expanse unfolded before the group, revealing celestial landscapes where cosmic energies intertwined with the threads of fate, creating a tapestry woven with the group's choices and the cosmic forces at play. In one celestial anomaly, the group encountered echoes of resilience—a potential future where the interconnected destinies weathered cosmic storms and emerged stronger. Symbols of revelation illuminated the astral surroundings, depicting a tapestry woven with fortitude, unity, and the unwavering spirit of the town's destiny.

In another anomaly, the group faced manifestations of vulnerability—a potential future where the threads of fate were tested by external forces. Symbols of revelation flickered with subtle energies, revealing the consequences of choices that left the interconnected destinies exposed to cosmic uncertainties. Guided by the guardian's echo, the group navigated through the celestial challenges, encountering cosmic puzzles and trials that tested their understanding of the ongoing dance of destinies. Symbols of revelation and interconnected destinies responded dynamically to their choices, reflecting the group's mastery over the cosmic forces that guided the threads of fate. In the heart of a celestial nexus, the group faced a manifestation of the astral currents—a convergence of cosmic forces that echoed with the consequences of their choices. Symbols of revelation and interconnected destinies pulsed with anticipation, inviting the group to reflect on the ongoing narrative within the intricate dance of destinies. With each reflection, the group deepened their understanding of the interconnected destinies and the profound impact of their choices within the astral realms. The guardian's echo, a harmonious cadence in the cosmic currents, acknowledged their evolving mastery over the cosmic forces and encouraged them to press on into the mysteries that awaited. As they moved through the celestial nexus, symbols of revelation and interconnected destinies continued to guide their path. The astral currents pulsed with cosmic energy, inviting the group to explore further revelations in the dark and unlock the true potential of the threads of fate within the ongoing cosmic tapestry. In the aftermath of the celestial nexus, the group felt a resonance with the cosmic forces, a harmonious connection that deepened their bond with the interconnected destinies. Symbols of revelation continued to glow with a radiant luminosity, signaling that the journey was far from over, and the mysteries that lay ahead in the astral realms awaited their exploration.

As the group advanced through the astral realms, the symbols of interconnected destinies continued to illuminate their path. The guardian's echo resonated with a subtle assurance, guiding them toward the heart of the cosmic tapestry, where the threads of fate converged with celestial energies. The astral expanse unfolded before them, revealing celestial anomalies that shimmered with the consequences of their journey. Symbols of revelation pulsed with an ethereal brilliance, offering glimpses into potential futures shaped by the interconnected destinies and the choices made in the ongoing dance of cosmic forces. In one celestial anomaly, the group witnessed echoes of connection—a potential future where the threads of fate were intricately woven, creating a tapestry of unity, understanding, and shared destiny. Symbols of revelation illuminated the astral surroundings, portraying a vision of the town flourishing in harmonious balance. In another anomaly, the group faced manifestations of disconnection—a potential future where the threads of fate unraveled in discord. Symbols of revelation flickered with disjointed energies, portraying the consequences of choices that strained the interconnected destinies and pushed the town toward the edge of cosmic isolation.

Guided by the guardian's echo, the group navigated through the celestial challenges, encountering cosmic puzzles and trials that tested their mastery over the dance of destinies. Symbols of revelation and interconnected destinies responded dynamically to their choices, reflecting the group's evolving understanding of the cosmic forces at play. In the heart of a celestial nexus, the group faced a manifestation of the astral currents—a convergence of cosmic forces that echoed with the consequences of their choices. Symbols of revelation and interconnected destinies pulsed with anticipation, inviting the group to reflect on the ongoing narrative within the intricate dance of destinies. With each reflection, the group deepened their connection to the interconnected destinies, recognizing the profound impact of their choices within the astral realms. The guardian's echo, a harmonious cadence in the cosmic currents, acknowledged their evolving mastery over the cosmic forces and encouraged them to press on into the mysteries that awaited. As they moved through the celestial nexus, symbols of revelation and interconnected destinies continued to guide their path. The astral currents pulsed with cosmic energy, inviting the group to explore further revelations in the dark and unlock the true potential of the threads of fate within the ongoing cosmic tapestry. In the aftermath of the celestial nexus, the group felt a resonance with the cosmic forces, a harmonious connection that deepened their bond with the interconnected destinies. Symbols of revelation continued to glow with a radiant luminosity, signaling that the journey was far from over, and the mysteries that lay ahead in the astral realms awaited their exploration. As the group ventured deeper into the astral realms, the symbols of interconnected destinies guided them through celestial anomalies, each pulsating with the consequences of their journey. The guardian's echo, a comforting presence in the cosmic currents, resonated with a profound understanding of the ongoing dance of destinies. Symbols of revelation pulsed with ethereal light, unveiling potential futures shaped by the threads of fate and the choices made by the group. The astral expanse unfolded before them, revealing cosmic landscapes where the interconnected destinies intertwined with celestial energies, creating a tapestry woven with the group's decisions and the cosmic forces at play. In one celestial anomaly, the group witnessed echoes of balance—a potential future where the threads of fate were delicately woven, creating a tapestry of equilibrium, cooperation, and shared purpose. Symbols of revelation illuminated the astral surroundings, portraying a vision of the town thriving in harmonious unity.

In another anomaly, the group faced manifestations of imbalance—a potential future where the threads of fate teetered on the edge of discord. Symbols of revelation flickered with chaotic energies, portraying the consequences of choices that disrupted the interconnected destinies and cast shadows over the town's cosmic equilibrium. Guided by the guardian's echo, the group navigated through celestial challenges, encountering cosmic puzzles and trials that tested their mastery over the dance of destinies. Symbols of revelation and interconnected destinies responded dynamically to their choices, reflecting the group's evolving understanding of the cosmic forces guiding the threads of fate. In the heart of a celestial nexus, the group faced a manifestation of the astral currents—a convergence of cosmic forces echoing with the consequences of their choices. Symbols of revelation and interconnected destinies pulsed with anticipation, inviting the group to reflect on the ongoing narrative within the intricate dance of destinies. With each reflection, the group deepened their connection to the interconnected destinies, acknowledging the far-reaching impact of their choices within the astral realms. The guardian's echo, a harmonious cadence in the cosmic currents, recognized their evolving mastery over the cosmic forces and encouraged them to press on into the mysteries that awaited. As they moved through the celestial nexus, symbols of revelation and interconnected destinies continued to guide their path. The astral currents pulsed with cosmic energy, inviting the group to explore further revelations in the dark and unlock the true potential of the threads of fate within the ongoing cosmic tapestry. In the aftermath of the celestial nexus, the group felt a resonance with the cosmic forces, a harmonious connection that deepened their bond with the interconnected destinies. Symbols of revelation continued to glow with a radiant luminosity, signaling that the journey was far from over, and the mysteries that lay ahead in the astral realms awaited their exploration.

# Chapter 11: Nature's Wrath

As the group delved deeper into the astral realms, the luminous symbols of interconnected destinies guided them toward a celestial convergence marked by an ominous cosmic resonance. The guardian's echo, now tinged with a sense of foreboding, urged them to approach Nature's Wrath with caution. The astral expanse unfolded before the group, revealing a landscape transformed by the forces of nature. Symbols of revelation pulsed with an intense energy, portraying potential futures where the threads of fate intertwined with the primal forces that governed the natural world. In one celestial anomaly, the group witnessed echoes of tranquility—a potential future where the interconnected destinies harmonized with nature's rhythms. Symbols of revelation illuminated the astral surroundings, portraying a vision of the town flourishing in symbiotic balance with the cosmic energies of the natural realm. In another anomaly, the group faced manifestations of upheaval—a potential future where the threads of fate were disrupted by the chaotic forces of nature. Symbols of revelation flickered with tempestuous energies, revealing the consequences of choices that angered the cosmic forces governing the delicate equilibrium. Guided by the guardian's echo, the group navigated through celestial challenges within Nature's Wrath, encountering cosmic storms, ethereal tempests, and manifestations of the untamed forces of the astral realms. Symbols of revelation and interconnected destinies responded dynamically to their choices, reflecting the group's ability to navigate the primal forces shaping the threads of fate. In the heart of a celestial nexus within Nature's Wrath, the group faced a manifestation of the astral currents—a convergence where the threads of fate intersected with the natural forces. Symbols of revelation and interconnected destinies pulsed with primal anticipation, inviting the group to reflect on the ongoing narrative within the intricate dance of destinies influenced by Nature's Wrath.

With each reflection, the group deepened their understanding of the interconnected destinies and the profound impact of their choices within the astral realms governed by nature's fury. The guardian's echo, a harmonious cadence in the cosmic currents, acknowledged their evolving mastery over the natural forces and encouraged them to press on into the mysteries that awaited. As they moved through the celestial nexus, symbols of revelation and interconnected destinies continued to guide their path. The astral currents pulsed with the untamed energy of Nature's Wrath, inviting the group to explore further revelations in the dark and unlock the true potential of the threads of fate within the ongoing cosmic tapestry shaped by the forces of nature. In the aftermath of the celestial nexus, the group felt the resonance of nature's energies, a harmonious connection that deepened their understanding of the interconnected destinies entwined with the natural forces. Symbols of revelation continued to glow with a primal luminosity, signaling that the journey through Nature's Wrath was a pivotal chapter in the ongoing exploration of the astral realms. And so, with the echoes of cosmic wisdom and the revelations within Nature's Wrath guiding their way, the group pressed on into the continuing cosmic tapestry. The interconnected destinies, now shaped by the primal forces of nature, awaited further unraveling in the intricate expanse of the astral realms.

As the group ventured further into Nature's Wrath, the celestial anomalies within the astral realms became more pronounced, reflecting the intricate dance of destinies influenced by the primal forces of nature. Symbols of revelation pulsed with vibrant energy, revealing potential futures where the threads of fate intertwined with the untamed essence of the natural world. In one celestial anomaly, the group witnessed echoes of symbiosis—a potential future where the interconnected destinies coexisted in harmony with the elemental forces. Symbols of revelation illuminated the astral surroundings, portraying a vision of the town flourishing amidst the cyclical rhythms of nature. In another anomaly, the group faced manifestations of discord—an ominous future where the threads of fate were thrown into disarray by the unrestrained fury of the natural forces. Symbols of revelation flickered with turbulent energies, exposing the consequences of choices that disrupted the delicate balance between the town's destiny and nature's wrath. Guided by the guardian's echo, the group navigated through celestial challenges within Nature's Wrath, encountering cosmic storms, ethereal tempests, and manifestations of the untamed forces of the astral realms. Symbols of revelation and interconnected destinies responded dynamically to their choices, reflecting the group's ability to navigate the primal forces shaping the threads of fate. In the heart of a celestial nexus within Nature's Wrath, the group faced a manifestation of the astral currents—a convergence where the threads of fate intersected with the natural forces. Symbols of revelation and interconnected destinies pulsed with primal anticipation, inviting the group to reflect on the ongoing narrative within the intricate dance of destinies influenced by Nature's Wrath. With each reflection, the group deepened their understanding of the interconnected destinies and the profound impact of their choices within the astral realms governed by nature's fury. The guardian's echo, a harmonious cadence in the cosmic currents, acknowledged their evolving mastery over the natural forces and encouraged them to press on into the mysteries that awaited. As they moved through the celestial nexus, symbols of revelation and interconnected destinies continued to guide their path. The astral currents pulsed with the untamed energy of Nature's Wrath, inviting the group to explore further revelations in the dark and unlock the true potential of the threads of fate within the ongoing cosmic tapestry shaped by the forces of nature.

In the aftermath of the celestial nexus, the group felt the resonance of nature's energies, a harmonious connection that deepened their understanding of the interconnected destinies entwined with the natural forces. Symbols of revelation continued to glow with a primal luminosity, signaling that the journey through Nature's Wrath was a pivotal chapter in the ongoing exploration of the astral realms. As the group continued their journey through Nature's Wrath, the astral realms unfolded with a tempestuous beauty. The guardian's echo, now interwoven with the primal forces, guided them through celestial anomalies that vividly portrayed the consequences of their choices within the natural tapestry of interconnected destinies. In one celestial anomaly, the group witnessed echoes of resilience—a potential future where the town's destiny stood strong against the elemental onslaught. Symbols of revelation illuminated the astral surroundings, portraying a vision of the community adapting and thriving amidst the challenges imposed by Nature's Wrath. In another anomaly, the group faced manifestations of vulnerability—an ominous future where the threads of fate quivered under the weight of nature's relentless force. Symbols of revelation flickered with subtle energies, revealing the consequences of choices that left the interconnected destinies exposed to the capricious whims of the astral tempest. Guided by the guardian's echo, the group navigated through celestial challenges, confronting cosmic storms, ethereal tempests, and manifestations of the untamed forces. Symbols of revelation and interconnected destinies responded dynamically to their choices, highlighting the group's ability to navigate the primal forces shaping the threads of fate. In the heart of a celestial nexus within Nature's Wrath, the group faced a manifestation of the astral currents—a convergence where the threads of fate intersected with the elemental forces. Symbols of revelation and interconnected destinies pulsed with primal anticipation, inviting the group to reflect on the ongoing narrative within the intricate dance of destinies influenced by Nature's Wrath. With each reflection, the group deepened their connection to the interconnected destinies, acknowledging the profound impact of their choices within the astral realms governed by nature's fury. The guardian's echo, a harmonious cadence in the cosmic currents, recognized their evolving mastery over the natural forces and encouraged them to press on into the mysteries that awaited. As they moved through the celestial nexus, symbols of revelation and interconnected destinies continued to guide their path. The astral currents pulsed with the untamed energy of Nature's Wrath, inviting the group to explore further revelations in the dark and unlock the true potential of the threads of fate within the ongoing cosmic tapestry shaped by the forces of nature. In the aftermath of the celestial nexus, the group felt the resonance of nature's energies, a harmonious connection that deepened their understanding of the interconnected destinies entwined with the natural forces. Symbols of revelation continued to glow with a primal luminosity, signaling that the journey through Nature's Wrath was a pivotal chapter in the ongoing exploration of the astral realms. As the group pressed on through Nature's Wrath, the celestial anomalies became more intense, reflecting the intricate dance of destinies entwined with the primal forces of the natural world. Symbols of revelation pulsed with dynamic energy, revealing potential futures where the threads of fate were interwoven with the untamed essence of the astral realms. In one celestial anomaly, the group witnessed echoes of adaptation—a potential future where the interconnected destinies evolved and embraced the wild energies surrounding them. Symbols of revelation illuminated the astral surroundings, portraying a vision of the town flourishing amidst the ever-changing dance of the elements.

In another anomaly, the group faced manifestations of resistance—an ominous future where the threads of fate strained against the relentless forces of Nature's Wrath. Symbols of revelation flickered with resilient energies, exposing the consequences of choices that sought to defy the natural order and disrupt the harmony within the cosmic tapestry. Guided by the guardian's echo, the group navigated through celestial challenges within Nature's Wrath, encountering cosmic storms, ethereal tempests, and manifestations of the untamed forces of the astral realms. Symbols of revelation and interconnected destinies responded dynamically to their choices, highlighting the group's ability to navigate the primal forces shaping the threads of fate. In the heart of a celestial nexus within Nature's Wrath, the group faced a manifestation of the astral currents—a convergence where the threads of fate intersected with the elemental forces. Symbols of revelation and interconnected destinies pulsed with primal anticipation, inviting the group to reflect on the ongoing narrative within the intricate dance of destinies influenced by Nature's Wrath. With each reflection, the group deepened their connection to the interconnected destinies, acknowledging the profound impact of their choices within the astral realms governed by nature's fury. The guardian's echo, a harmonious cadence in the cosmic currents, recognized their evolving mastery over the natural forces and encouraged them to press on into the mysteries that awaited. As they moved through the celestial nexus, symbols of revelation and interconnected destinies continued to guide their path. The astral currents pulsed with the untamed energy of Nature's Wrath, inviting the group to explore further revelations in the dark and unlock the true potential of the threads of fate within the ongoing cosmic tapestry shaped by the forces of nature. In the aftermath of the celestial nexus, the group felt the resonance of nature's energies, a harmonious connection that deepened their understanding of the interconnected destinies entwined with the natural forces. Symbols of revelation continued to glow with a primal luminosity, signaling that the journey through Nature's Wrath was a pivotal chapter in the ongoing exploration of the astral realms.

The group, now accustomed to the rhythmic cadence of Nature's Wrath, ventured deeper into the astral realms, where the celestial anomalies took on an even more profound significance. Symbols of revelation pulsed with an intense energy, revealing potential futures where the threads of fate harmonized with the primal forces of the natural world. In one celestial anomaly, the group witnessed echoes of coexistence—a potential future where the interconnected destinies seamlessly integrated with the elemental energies surrounding them. Symbols of revelation illuminated the astral surroundings, portraying a vision of the town thriving in a symbiotic dance with the untamed forces of Nature's Wrath. In another anomaly, the group faced manifestations of upheaval—an ominous future where the threads of fate were thrust into chaos by the unrestrained fury of the natural forces. Symbols of revelation flickered with turbulent energies, exposing the consequences of choices that disrupted the delicate equilibrium between the town's destiny and the relentless power of the astral tempest. Guided by the guardian's echo, the group navigated through celestial challenges within Nature's Wrath, encountering cosmic storms, ethereal tempests, and manifestations of the untamed forces of the astral realms. Symbols of revelation and interconnected destinies responded dynamically to their choices, highlighting the group's ability to navigate the primal forces shaping the threads of fate. In the heart of a celestial nexus within Nature's Wrath, the group faced a manifestation of the astral currents—a convergence where the threads of fate intersected with the elemental forces. Symbols of revelation and interconnected destinies pulsed with primal anticipation, inviting the group to reflect on the ongoing narrative within the intricate dance of destinies influenced by Nature's Wrath.

With each reflection, the group deepened their connection to the interconnected destinies, acknowledging the profound impact of their choices within the astral realms governed by nature's fury. The guardian's echo, a harmonious cadence in the cosmic currents, recognized their evolving mastery over the natural forces and encouraged them to press on into the mysteries that awaited. As they moved through the celestial nexus, symbols of revelation and interconnected destinies continued to guide their path. The astral currents pulsed with the untamed energy of Nature's Wrath, inviting the group to explore further revelations in the dark and unlock the true potential of the threads of fate within the ongoing cosmic tapestry shaped by the forces of nature. In the aftermath of the celestial nexus, the group felt the resonance of nature's energies, a harmonious connection that deepened their understanding of the interconnected destinies entwined with the natural forces. Symbols of revelation continued to glow with a primal luminosity, signaling that the journey through Nature's Wrath was a pivotal chapter in the ongoing exploration of the astral realms.

As the group navigated further through Nature's Wrath, the celestial anomalies grew more intense, each revealing potential futures influenced by the intricate dance of destinies with the primal forces of the natural world. Symbols of revelation pulsed with vibrant energy, portraying a vivid tapestry where the threads of fate intertwined with the untamed essence of the astral realms. In one celestial anomaly, the group witnessed echoes of equilibrium—a potential future where the interconnected destinies achieved a delicate balance with the elemental energies. Symbols of revelation illuminated the astral surroundings, portraying a vision of the town flourishing amidst the ever-shifting dance of the elements. In another anomaly, the group faced manifestations of imbalance—an ominous future where the threads of fate teetered on the brink of discord under the relentless forces of Nature's Wrath. Symbols of revelation flickered with tumultuous energies, exposing the consequences of choices that disrupted the cosmic equilibrium between the town's destiny and the powerful astral tempest. Guided by the guardian's echo, the group navigated through celestial challenges within Nature's Wrath, confronting cosmic storms, ethereal tempests, and manifestations of the untamed forces of the astral realms. Symbols of revelation and interconnected destinies responded dynamically to their choices, demonstrating the group's growing mastery over the primal forces shaping the threads of fate. In the heart of a celestial nexus within Nature's Wrath, the group faced a manifestation of the astral currents—a convergence where the threads of fate intersected with the elemental forces. Symbols of revelation and interconnected destinies pulsed with primal anticipation, inviting the group to reflect on the ongoing narrative within the intricate dance of destinies influenced by Nature's Wrath. With each reflection, the group deepened their connection to the interconnected destinies, acknowledging the profound impact of their choices within the astral realms governed by nature's fury. The guardian's echo, a harmonious cadence in the cosmic currents, recognized their evolving mastery over the natural forces and encouraged them to press on into the mysteries that awaited.

As they moved through the celestial nexus, symbols of revelation and interconnected destinies continued to guide their path. The astral currents pulsed with the untamed energy of Nature's Wrath, inviting the group to explore further revelations in the dark and unlock the true potential of the threads of fate within the ongoing cosmic tapestry shaped by the forces of nature. In the aftermath of the celestial nexus, the group felt the resonance of nature's energies, a harmonious connection that deepened their understanding of the interconnected destinies entwined with the natural forces. Symbols of revelation continued to glow with a primal luminosity, signaling that the journey through Nature's Wrath was a pivotal chapter in the ongoing exploration of the astral realms.

As the group delved deeper into Nature's Wrath, the astral realms seemed to echo with the tumultuous energies of the natural forces. Celestial anomalies continued to unveil potential futures, each painting a different facet of the ongoing dance of destinies with the primal forces of the environment. Symbols of revelation pulsed with an intensity that mirrored the ebb and flow of the elemental energies. In one celestial anomaly, the group witnessed echoes of resilience—a potential future where the interconnected destinies stood firm against the relentless onslaught of Nature's Wrath. Symbols of revelation illuminated the astral surroundings, portraying a vision of the town adapting and thriving amidst the ever-changing landscape of the astral tempest. In another anomaly, the group faced manifestations of fragility—an ominous future where the threads of fate trembled under the overwhelming force of the natural elements. Symbols of revelation flickered with delicate energies, revealing the consequences of choices that left the interconnected destinies vulnerable to the capricious whims of the astral storm. Guided by the guardian's echo, the group navigated through celestial challenges within Nature's Wrath, encountering cosmic storms, ethereal tempests, and manifestations of the untamed forces of the astral realms. Symbols of revelation and interconnected destinies responded dynamically to their choices, showcasing the group's increasing prowess in navigating the primal forces that shaped the threads of fate. In the heart of a celestial nexus within Nature's Wrath, the group faced a manifestation of the astral currents—a convergence where the threads of fate intersected with the elemental forces. Symbols of revelation and interconnected destinies pulsed with primal anticipation, inviting the group to reflect on the ongoing narrative within the intricate dance of destinies influenced by Nature's Wrath. With each reflection, the group deepened their connection to the interconnected destinies, recognizing the profound impact of their choices within the astral realms governed by nature's fury. The guardian's echo, a harmonious cadence in the cosmic currents, acknowledged their evolving mastery over the natural forces and encouraged them to press on into the mysteries that awaited.

As they moved through the celestial nexus, symbols of revelation and interconnected destinies continued to guide their path. The astral currents pulsed with the untamed energy of Nature's Wrath, inviting the group to explore further revelations in the dark and unlock the true potential of the threads of fate within the ongoing cosmic tapestry shaped by the forces of nature. In the aftermath of the celestial nexus, the group felt the resonance of nature's energies, a harmonious connection that deepened their understanding of the interconnected destinies entwined with the natural forces. Symbols of revelation continued to glow with a primal luminosity, signaling that the journey through Nature's Wrath was a pivotal chapter in the ongoing exploration of the astral realms.

# Chapter 12: Betrayal Unveiled

The group, having weathered the tempests of Nature's Wrath, continued their journey through the astral realms. However, as they progressed, an unsettling tension began to weave its way through the interconnected destinies. Whispers of betrayal lingered in the cosmic currents, and shadows of doubt cast themselves upon the once-united group. In the aftermath of the celestial nexus within Nature's Wrath, a revelation unfolded, revealing a betrayal that had been shrouded in secrecy. The guardian's echo, now tinged with sorrow, hinted at the fractures within the group's unity, as choices made in the face of adversity had consequences that rippled through the threads of fate. Symbols of revelation pulsated with a disconcerting glow, illustrating potential futures where trust was betrayed, alliances shattered, and the once-solid foundation of the group now stood on precarious ground. The astral expanse reflected the internal turmoil, with cosmic energies resonating with the echoes of deceit. As the group traversed through the astral realms, the guardian's echo guided them towards a pivotal moment—a convergence marked by the unveiling of the betrayal. The celestial anomalies whispered of hidden motives, clandestine actions, and the gradual erosion of the trust that had bound the destinies together. In one celestial anomaly, the group witnessed echoes of confrontation—a potential future where the threads of fate clashed in the wake of the revealed betrayal. Symbols of revelation illuminated the astral surroundings, portraying a vision of conflict that threatened to tear the interconnected destinies asunder. In another anomaly, the group faced manifestations of regret—an ominous future where the threads of fate were weighed down by the consequences of choices that led to the betrayal. Symbols of revelation flickered with somber energies, exposing the profound impact of actions that had fractured the bonds of trust within the cosmic tapestry. Guided by the guardian's echo, the group navigated through the turbulent astral currents, confronting cosmic challenges that mirrored the internal struggles of the group. Symbols of revelation and interconnected destinies responded dynamically to their choices, showcasing the group's resilience in the face of the betrayal that threatened to unravel the fabric of their shared destiny.

As the group approached the heart of the celestial nexus, the shadows of betrayal loomed large. Symbols of revelation and interconnected destinies pulsed with an ominous anticipation, inviting the group to confront the unveiled treachery and decide the fate of their collective journey. With each reflection, the group grappled with the revelation, recognizing the necessity of unity in the face of internal discord. The guardian's echo, a mournful cadence in the cosmic currents, urged them to find a path forward, where redemption and forgiveness could mend the frayed threads of trust within the astral tapestry. And so, as the group stood on the precipice of Betrayal Unveiled, the destiny of the interconnected individuals hung in the balance. The choices made in the wake of this revelation would shape not only their shared future but also the resilience of the bonds that had once bound them together in the intricate dance of destinies. In the somber aftermath of the betrayal's revelation, the group grappled with the echoes of discord that permeated the once-unified destinies. Symbols of revelation pulsed with an unsettling glow, reflecting the fractures within the astral tapestry as the weight of betrayal cast a shadow over their collective journey. As the group moved through the astral realms, the guardian's echo guided them toward a convergence marked by the consequences of the unveiled treachery. The celestial anomalies painted vivid portraits of potential futures, each illustrating the aftermath of the betrayal and the divergent paths the interconnected destinies could now take. In one celestial anomaly, the group witnessed echoes of reconciliation—a potential future where the threads of fate, though strained, found a way to mend the bonds of trust. Symbols of revelation illuminated the astral surroundings, portraying a vision of unity born from the crucible of betrayal, where forgiveness and understanding prevailed. In another anomaly, the group faced manifestations of estrangement—an ominous future where the threads of fate unraveled further, leading to irreparable divisions within the once-tight-knit group. Symbols of revelation flickered with dissonant energies, exposing the consequences of choices that fueled the flames of discord. Guided by the guardian's echo, the group navigated through celestial challenges, confronting cosmic storms that mirrored the internal tempests of emotions. Symbols of revelation and interconnected destinies responded dynamically to their choices, showcasing the group's resilience in the face of the betrayal that threatened to sever the ties that bound them. In the heart of the celestial nexus, the group confronted a manifestation of the astral currents—a convergence where the threads of fate intersected with the consequences of the unveiled betrayal. Symbols of revelation and interconnected destinies pulsed with a tense anticipation, inviting the group to reflect on the ongoing narrative within the intricate dance of destinies influenced by the aftermath of the betrayal. With each reflection, the group grappled with the complexities of trust, loyalty, and the delicate nature of human connections. The guardian's echo, a melancholic cadence in the cosmic currents, encouraged them to consider the paths before them and the potential for redemption within the astral tapestry.

As they moved through the celestial nexus, symbols of revelation and interconnected destinies continued to guide their path. The astral currents pulsed with the lingering energy of the betrayal, inviting the group to explore further revelations in the dark and determine the true resilience of their collective journey. In the aftermath of the celestial nexus, the group felt the weight of their choices, aware that the destiny of the interconnected individuals hung in the balance. The guardian's echo, now a guide through the shadows of their own making, urged them to navigate the intricate expanse of the astral realms with a renewed sense of purpose, seeking to weave a new chapter in the tapestry of their shared destiny—one shaped by forgiveness, redemption, and the strength to overcome the echoes of betrayal.

As the group ventured further into the astral realms, the aftermath of the betrayal lingered like a shadow over their interconnected destinies. The celestial anomalies continued to unfold potential futures, each revealing the consequences of their choices in the wake of the unveiled treachery. Symbols of revelation pulsed with a delicate balance, teetering between redemption and further discord. In one celestial anomaly, the group witnessed echoes of forgiveness—a potential future where the threads of fate, though frayed, found a path to healing. Symbols of revelation illuminated the astral surroundings, portraying a vision of unity born from the crucible of betrayal, where understanding and compassion prevailed over the wounds inflicted. In another anomaly, the group faced manifestations of stubbornness—an ominous future where the threads of fate remained strained, as the echoes of the betrayal hardened hearts and deepened the chasms within the group. Symbols of revelation flickered with stubborn energies, exposing the consequences of choices that resisted the path of reconciliation. Guided by the guardian's echo, the group navigated through celestial challenges, confronting cosmic storms that mirrored the internal tempests of emotions. Symbols of revelation and interconnected destinies responded dynamically to their choices, showcasing the group's resilience in the face of the betrayal that threatened to sever the ties that bound them. In the heart of the celestial nexus, the group confronted a manifestation of the astral currents—a convergence where the threads of fate intersected with the consequences of the unveiled betrayal. Symbols of revelation and interconnected destinies pulsed with a tense anticipation, inviting the group to reflect on the ongoing narrative within the intricate dance of destinies influenced by the aftermath of the betrayal. With each reflection, the group grappled with the complexities of trust, loyalty, and the delicate nature of human connections. The guardian's echo, a melancholic cadence in the cosmic currents, encouraged them to consider the paths before them and the potential for redemption within the astral tapestry. As they moved through the celestial nexus, symbols of revelation and interconnected destinies continued to guide their path. The astral currents pulsed with the lingering energy of the betrayal, inviting the group to explore further revelations in the dark and determine the true resilience of their collective journey. In the aftermath of the celestial nexus, the group felt the weight of their choices, aware that the destiny of the interconnected individuals hung in the balance. The guardian's echo, now a guide through the shadows of their own making, urged them to navigate the intricate expanse of the astral realms with a renewed sense of purpose, seeking to weave a new chapter in the tapestry of their shared destiny—one shaped by forgiveness, redemption, and the strength to overcome the echoes of betrayal.

As the group forged ahead, the astral realms seemed to echo with the unresolved emotions lingering from the betrayal. The guardian's echo, now a gentle melody tinged with both sadness and hope, guided them towards the next celestial convergence—a place where the threads of fate intersected with the group's collective response to the revealed treachery. In one celestial anomaly, the group witnessed echoes of redemption—a potential future where the threads of fate, once strained, found a path to renewal. Symbols of revelation illuminated the astral surroundings, portraying a vision of the group collectively working towards healing the wounds inflicted by the betrayal.

Forgiveness and understanding became the guiding lights in this potential future. In another anomaly, the group faced manifestations of defiance—an ominous future where the threads of fate remained tangled in resentment, as some resisted the call for reconciliation. Symbols of revelation flickered with discordant energies, exposing the consequences of choices that fueled the flames of internal conflict. Guided by the guardian's echo, the group navigated through celestial challenges, confronting cosmic storms that mirrored the internal tempests of emotions. Symbols of revelation and interconnected destinies responded dynamically to their choices, showcasing the group's resilience in the face of the betrayal that threatened to sever the ties that bound them. In the heart of the celestial nexus, the group confronted a manifestation of the astral currents—a convergence where the threads of fate intersected with the consequences of the unveiled betrayal. Symbols of revelation and interconnected destinies pulsed with a tense anticipation, inviting the group to reflect on the ongoing narrative within the intricate dance of destinies influenced by the aftermath of the betrayal. With each reflection, the group grappled with the complexities of trust, loyalty, and the delicate nature of human connections. The guardian's echo, a melancholic cadence in the cosmic currents, encouraged them to consider the paths before them and the potential for redemption within the astral tapestry. As they moved through the celestial nexus, symbols of revelation and interconnected destinies continued to guide their path. The astral currents pulsed with the lingering energy of the betrayal, inviting the group to explore further revelations in the dark and determine the true resilience of their collective journey. In the aftermath of the celestial nexus, the group felt the weight of their choices, aware that the destiny of the interconnected individuals hung in the balance. The guardian's echo, now a guide through the shadows of their own making, urged them to navigate the intricate expanse of the astral realms with a renewed sense of purpose, seeking to weave a new chapter in the tapestry of their shared destiny—one shaped by forgiveness, redemption, and the strength to overcome the echoes of betrayal.

As the group moved forward, the astral tapestry seemed to weave a delicate dance between reconciliation and continued strife. The guardian's echo, a poignant melody in the cosmic currents, guided them through the celestial anomalies that unfolded potential futures influenced by their response to the betrayal. In one celestial anomaly, the group witnessed echoes of healing—a potential future where the threads of fate, though scarred by the betrayal, found a way to mend. Symbols of revelation illuminated the astral surroundings, portraying a vision of the group collectively working towards rebuilding trust and forging a new path forward. In another anomaly, the group faced manifestations of stubbornness—an ominous future where the threads of fate remained entangled in resentment. Symbols of revelation flickered with discordant energies, exposing the consequences of choices that resisted the call for reconciliation, perpetuating the rift within the interconnected destinies. Guided by the guardian's echo, the group navigated through celestial challenges, confronting cosmic storms that mirrored the internal tempests of emotions. Symbols of revelation and interconnected destinies responded dynamically to their choices, showcasing the group's resilience in the face of the betrayal that threatened to sever the ties that bound them. In the heart of the celestial nexus, the group confronted a manifestation of the astral currents—a convergence where the threads of fate intersected with the consequences of the unveiled betrayal. Symbols of revelation and interconnected destinies pulsed with a tense anticipation, inviting the group to reflect on the ongoing narrative within the intricate dance of destinies influenced by the aftermath of the betrayal. With each reflection, the group grappled with the complexities of trust, loyalty, and the delicate nature of human connections. The guardian's echo, a melancholic cadence in the cosmic currents, encouraged them to consider the paths before them and the potential for redemption within the astral tapestry. As they moved through the celestial nexus, symbols of revelation and interconnected destinies continued to guide their path. The astral currents pulsed with the lingering energy of the betrayal, inviting the group to explore further revelations in the dark and determine the true resilience of their collective journey. In the aftermath of the celestial nexus, the group felt the weight of their choices, aware that the destiny of the interconnected individuals hung in the balance. The guardian's echo, now a guide through the shadows of their own making, urged them to navigate the intricate expanse of the astral realms with a renewed sense of purpose, seeking to weave a new chapter in the tapestry of their shared destiny—one shaped by forgiveness, redemption, and the strength to overcome the echoes of betrayal. And so, with the echoes of discord lingering in the cosmic currents, the group pressed on into the continuing cosmic tapestry, each step a testament to their resilience and the ongoing evolution of the interconnected destinies in the aftermath of the unveiled betrayal.

# Chapter 13: Desperation Sets In

As the group ventured deeper into the astral realms, the lingering echoes of betrayal cast a palpable shadow over their interconnected destinies. The guardian's echo, now a mournful melody, guided them towards a new convergence—a place where the threads of fate intersected with the growing desperation within the group. In one celestial anomaly, the group witnessed echoes of conflict—a potential future where the threads of fate unraveled further as desperation fueled internal strife. Symbols of revelation illuminated the astral surroundings, portraying a vision of the group succumbing to the weight of their circumstances, each individual driven by their own desperate motivations. In another anomaly, the group faced manifestations of isolation—an ominous future where the threads of fate fragmented as desperation led individuals to pursue their survival at the expense of unity. Symbols of revelation flickered with solitary energies, exposing the consequences of choices that severed the bonds that once held the destinies together. Guided by the guardian's echo, the group navigated through celestial challenges, confronting cosmic storms that mirrored the internal tempests of emotions. Symbols of revelation and interconnected destinies responded dynamically to their choices, showcasing the group's resilience but also the escalating desperation that threatened to consume them. In the heart of the celestial nexus, the group confronted a manifestation of the astral currents—a convergence where the threads of fate intersected with the consequences of growing desperation. Symbols of revelation and interconnected destinies pulsed with an ominous anticipation, inviting the group to reflect on the ongoing narrative within the intricate dance of destinies influenced by their escalating struggles.

With each reflection, the group grappled with the intensifying desperation, recognizing the precarious nature of their situation. The guardian's echo, a haunting cadence in the cosmic currents, urged them to confront the shadows within themselves and each other, to find a way forward amidst the encroaching darkness. As they moved through the celestial nexus, symbols of revelation and interconnected destinies continued to guide their path. The astral currents pulsed with the energy of desperation, urging the group to explore further revelations in the dark and to discover the true extent of their collective resilience in the face of adversity. In the aftermath of the celestial nexus, the group felt the weight of desperation settling in, aware that the destiny of the interconnected individuals hung in the balance. The guardian's echo, now a somber companion through the trials of their own making, encouraged them to navigate the intricate expanse of the astral realms with newfound determination, seeking to weave a new chapter in the tapestry of their shared destiny—one shaped by resilience, unity, and the strength to overcome the encroaching desperation. As the group delved deeper into the astral realms, the fabric of their interconnected destinies began to fray under the weight of growing desperation. The guardian's echo, a haunting refrain, guided them through the tumultuous celestial anomalies that unfolded potential futures shaped by their response to the encroaching darkness. In one celestial anomaly, the group witnessed echoes of sacrifice—a potential future where the threads of fate, strained by desperation, found a glimmer of hope through selflessness. Symbols of revelation illuminated the astral surroundings, portraying a vision of individuals making sacrifices for the greater good, even as the shadows of despair threatened to consume them. In another anomaly, the group faced manifestations of recklessness—an ominous future where the threads of fate spiraled into chaos as desperation drove impulsive actions. Symbols of revelation flickered with erratic energies, exposing the consequences of choices made in haste, each decision pushing the group further into the clutches of despair.

Guided by the guardian's echo, the group navigated through celestial challenges, confronting cosmic storms that mirrored the internal tempests of emotions. Symbols of revelation and interconnected destinies responded dynamically to their choices, showcasing the group's resilience but also the escalating desperation that threatened to engulf them. In the heart of the celestial nexus, the group confronted a manifestation of the astral currents—a convergence where the threads of fate intersected with the consequences of growing desperation. Symbols of revelation and interconnected destinies pulsed with an ominous anticipation, inviting the group to reflect on the ongoing narrative within the intricate dance of destinies influenced by their escalating struggles. With each reflection, the group grappled with the intensifying desperation, recognizing the precarious nature of their situation. The guardian's echo, a haunting cadence in the cosmic currents, urged them to confront the shadows within themselves and each other, to find a way forward amidst the encroaching darkness. As they moved through the celestial nexus, symbols of revelation and interconnected destinies continued to guide their path. The astral currents pulsed with the energy of desperation, urging the group to explore further revelations in the dark and to discover the true extent of their collective resilience in the face of adversity. In the aftermath of the celestial nexus, the group felt the weight of desperation settling in, aware that the destiny of the interconnected individuals hung in the balance. The guardian's echo, now a somber companion through the trials of their own making, encouraged them to navigate the intricate expanse of the astral realms with newfound determination, seeking to weave a new chapter in the tapestry of their shared destiny—one shaped by resilience, unity, and the strength to overcome the encroaching desperation.

As the group forged ahead through the astral realms, the resonance of desperation echoed in the cosmic currents, creating an atmosphere fraught with uncertainty. The guardian's echo, now a haunting melody that seemed to mirror the group's inner turmoil, guided them through the celestial anomalies that unfolded potential futures shaped by their response to the growing desperation. In one celestial anomaly, the group witnessed echoes of unity—a potential future where the threads of fate, though strained, found strength through collective determination. Symbols of revelation illuminated the astral surroundings, portraying a vision of the group standing resilient against the encroaching darkness, each member supporting the other in the face of desperation. In another anomaly, the group faced manifestations of despair—an ominous future where the threads of fate unraveled as hope waned in the face of escalating desperation. Symbols of revelation flickered with somber energies, exposing the consequences of choices that succumbed to the shadows, leaving the group vulnerable to the abyss of despair. Guided by the guardian's echo, the group navigated through celestial challenges, confronting cosmic storms that mirrored the internal tempests of emotions. Symbols of revelation and interconnected destinies responded dynamically to their choices, showcasing the group's resilience but also the delicate balance they had to maintain in the midst of desperation.

In the heart of the celestial nexus, the group confronted a manifestation of the astral currents—a convergence where the threads of fate intersected with the consequences of growing desperation. Symbols of revelation and interconnected destinies pulsed with an ominous anticipation, inviting the group to reflect on the ongoing narrative within the intricate dance of destinies influenced by their escalating struggles. With each reflection, the group grappled with the intensifying desperation, recognizing the precarious nature of their situation. The guardian's echo, a haunting cadence in the cosmic currents, urged them to confront the shadows within themselves and each other, to find a way forward amidst the encroaching darkness. As they moved through the celestial nexus, symbols of revelation and interconnected destinies continued to guide their path. The astral currents pulsed with the energy of desperation, urging the group to explore further revelations in the dark and to discover the true extent of their collective resilience in the face of adversity.

In the aftermath of the celestial nexus, the group felt the weight of desperation settling in, aware that the destiny of the interconnected individuals hung in the balance. The guardian's echo, now a somber companion through the trials of their own making, encouraged them to navigate the intricate expanse of the astral realms with newfound determination, seeking to weave a new chapter in the tapestry of their shared destiny—one shaped by resilience, unity, and the strength to overcome the encroaching desperation.

As the group pressed on through the astral realms, the atmosphere thick with desperation, the guardian's echo guided them to a place where the threads of fate intersected with the dire consequences of their escalating struggles. In one celestial anomaly, the group witnessed echoes of determination—a potential future where the threads of fate, though strained, were fortified by the collective determination of the individuals. Symbols of revelation illuminated the astral surroundings, portraying a vision of the group pushing back against the encroaching darkness, fueled by a shared commitment to overcome the challenges born from desperation. In another anomaly, the group faced manifestations of hopelessness—an ominous future where the threads of fate unraveled as despair took hold. Symbols of revelation flickered with somber energies, exposing the consequences of choices that succumbed to the shadows, leaving the group vulnerable to the abyss of hopelessness. Guided by the guardian's echo, the group navigated through celestial challenges, confronting cosmic storms that mirrored the internal tempests of emotions. Symbols of revelation and interconnected destinies responded dynamically to their choices, showcasing the group's resilience but also the delicate balance they had to maintain in the midst of desperation. In the heart of the celestial nexus, the group confronted a manifestation of the astral currents—a convergence where the threads of fate intersected with the consequences of growing desperation. Symbols of revelation and interconnected destinies pulsed with an ominous anticipation, inviting the group to reflect on the ongoing narrative within the intricate dance of destinies influenced by their escalating struggles. With each reflection, the group grappled with the intensifying desperation, recognizing the precarious nature of their situation. The guardian's echo, a haunting cadence in the cosmic currents, urged them to confront the shadows within themselves and each other, to find a way forward amidst the encroaching darkness. As they moved through the celestial nexus, symbols of revelation and interconnected destinies continued to guide their path. The astral currents pulsed with the energy of desperation, urging the group to explore further revelations in the dark and to discover the true extent of their collective resilience in the face of adversity. In the aftermath of the celestial nexus, the group felt the weight of desperation settling in, aware that the destiny of the interconnected individuals hung in the balance. The guardian's echo, now a somber companion through the trials of their own making, encouraged them to navigate the intricate expanse of the astral realms with newfound determination, seeking to weave a new chapter in the tapestry of their shared destiny—one shaped by resilience, unity, and the strength to overcome the encroaching desperation.

As the group ventured further into the astral realms, the echoes of determination and hopelessness intertwined in the cosmic currents, creating a tense backdrop for the unfolding narrative of their interconnected destinies. The guardian's echo, a haunting melody that mirrored the group's internal struggles, guided them through the celestial anomalies. Each step forward was a delicate dance between resilience and vulnerability, as the consequences of their choices became more pronounced in the face of escalating desperation. In one celestial anomaly, the group witnessed echoes of sacrifice—a potential future where the threads of fate, strained by desperation, found strength through selfless acts. Symbols of revelation illuminated the astral surroundings, portraying a vision of individuals making sacrifices for the greater good, even as the shadows of despair threatened to engulf them. In another anomaly, the group faced manifestations of division—an ominous future where the threads of fate splintered under the weight of individual desperation. Symbols of revelation flickered with dissonant energies, exposing the consequences of choices that drove wedges between the members, fracturing the unity that once bound them. Guided by the guardian's echo, the group continued to navigate through celestial challenges, confronting cosmic storms that mirrored the internal tempests of emotions. Symbols of revelation and interconnected destinies responded dynamically to their choices, showcasing the delicate balance they had to maintain in the face of the escalating desperation that threatened to unravel the fabric of their collective journey. In the heart of the celestial nexus, the group confronted a manifestation of the astral currents—a convergence where the threads of fate intersected with the consequences of growing desperation. Symbols of revelation and interconnected destinies pulsed with an ominous anticipation, inviting the group to reflect on the ongoing narrative within the intricate dance of destinies influenced by their escalating struggles. With each reflection, the group grappled with the intensifying desperation, recognizing the precarious nature of their situation. The guardian's echo, a haunting cadence in the cosmic currents, urged them to confront the shadows within themselves and each other, to find a way forward amidst the encroaching darkness. As they moved through the celestial nexus, symbols of revelation and interconnected destinies continued to guide their path. The astral currents pulsed with the energy of desperation, urging the group to explore further revelations in the dark and to discover the true extent of their collective resilience in the face of adversity.

In the aftermath of the celestial nexus, the group felt the weight of desperation settling in, aware that the destiny of the interconnected individuals hung in the balance. The guardian's echo, now a somber companion through the trials of their own making, encouraged them to navigate the intricate expanse of the astral realms with newfound determination, seeking to weave a new chapter in the tapestry of their shared destiny—one shaped by resilience, unity, and the strength to overcome the encroaching desperation.

# Chapter 14: Shattered Alliances

As the group journeyed through the astral realms, the threads of fate seemed to tremble under the weight of their growing desperation. The guardian's echo, now a mournful refrain, guided them towards a new convergence—a place where the interconnected destinies would face a critical juncture. In one celestial anomaly, the group witnessed echoes of confrontation—a potential future where the threads of fate unraveled further as desperation fueled internal strife. Symbols of revelation illuminated the astral surroundings, portraying a vision of alliances shattering, each member driven by their own desperate motivations, blurring the lines between friend and foe. In another anomaly, the group faced manifestations of betrayal—an ominous future where the threads of fate fractured as desperation led to acts of treachery within the once-unified group. Symbols of revelation flickered with dissonant energies, exposing the consequences of choices that betrayed the trust that had bound the destinies together. Guided by the guardian's echo, the group navigated through celestial challenges, confronting cosmic storms that mirrored the internal tempests of emotions. Symbols of revelation and interconnected destinies responded dynamically to their choices, showcasing the group's resilience but also the escalating desperation that threatened to fracture the bonds they had forged. In the heart of the celestial nexus, the group confronted a manifestation of the astral currents—a convergence where the threads of fate intersected with the consequences of shattered alliances. Symbols of revelation and interconnected destinies pulsed with a foreboding intensity, inviting the group to reflect on the ongoing narrative within the intricate dance of destinies influenced by their escalating struggles. With each reflection, the group grappled with the intensifying desperation, recognizing the precarious nature of their situation. The guardian's echo, a haunting cadence in the cosmic currents, urged them to confront the shadows within themselves and each other, to find a way forward amidst the encroaching darkness. As they moved through the celestial nexus, symbols of revelation and interconnected destinies continued to guide their path. The astral currents pulsed with the energy of desperation, urging the group to explore further revelations in the dark and to discover the true extent of their collective resilience in the face of adversity. In the aftermath of the celestial nexus, the group felt the weight of desperation settling in, aware that the destiny of the interconnected individuals hung in the balance. The guardian's echo, now a somber companion through the trials of their own making, encouraged them to navigate the intricate expanse of the astral realms with newfound determination, seeking to weave a new chapter in the tapestry of their shared destiny—one shaped by resilience, unity, and the strength to overcome the encroaching desperation.

As the group traversed the astral realms, the resonance of desperation continued to weave a somber tapestry of intertwined destinies. The guardian's echo, now a haunting melody, guided them to a pivotal convergence—a moment where the threads of fate stood on the precipice of irreparable fracture. In one celestial anomaly, the group witnessed echoes of suspicion—a potential future where the threads of fate unraveled as desperation fueled mistrust among the once-unified individuals. Symbols of revelation illuminated the astral surroundings, portraying a vision of alliances shattering, each member haunted by doubt and suspicion, their unity now fragile and fractured. In another anomaly, the group faced manifestations of abandonment—an ominous future where the threads of fate fragmented as desperation led individuals to forsake their companions in a bid for personal survival. Symbols of revelation flickered with isolating energies, exposing the consequences of choices that severed the bonds that once held the destinies together. Guided by the guardian's echo, the group navigated through celestial challenges, confronting cosmic storms that mirrored the internal tempests of emotions. Symbols of revelation and interconnected destinies responded dynamically to their choices, showcasing the group's resilience but also the delicate balance they had to maintain in the face of the escalating desperation that threatened to tear them apart. In the heart of the celestial nexus, the group confronted a manifestation of the astral currents—a convergence where the threads of fate intersected with the consequences of shattered alliances. Symbols of revelation and interconnected destinies pulsed with a foreboding intensity, inviting the group to reflect on the ongoing narrative within the intricate dance of destinies influenced by their escalating struggles.

With each reflection, the group grappled with the intensifying desperation, recognizing the precarious nature of their situation. The guardian's echo, a haunting cadence in the cosmic currents, urged them to confront the shadows within themselves and each other, to find a way forward amidst the encroaching darkness. As they moved through the celestial nexus, symbols of revelation and interconnected destinies continued to guide their path. The astral currents pulsed with the energy of desperation, urging the group to explore further revelations in the dark and to discover the true extent of their collective resilience in the face of adversity. In the aftermath of the celestial nexus, the group felt the weight of desperation settling in, aware that the destiny of the interconnected individuals hung in the balance. The guardian's echo, now a somber companion through the trials of their own making, encouraged them to navigate the intricate expanse of the astral realms with newfound determination, seeking to weave a new chapter in the tapestry of their shared destiny—one shaped by resilience, unity, and the strength to overcome the encroaching desperation. And so, with the echoes of suspicion and abandonment resonating in the cosmic currents, the group pressed on into the continuing cosmic tapestry, each step a testament to their resolve and the evolving nature of the interconnected destinies in the face of escalating desperation and the specter of shattered alliances.

The group pressed forward, their journey through the astral realms fraught with the echoes of suspicion and the looming threat of shattered alliances. The guardian's echo, a mournful melody weaving through the cosmic currents, guided them toward a celestial crossroads where the destinies of the group hung in precarious balance. In one celestial anomaly, the group confronted echoes of reconciliation—a potential future where the threads of fate, though strained, found a way to mend through mutual understanding and shared burdens. Symbols of revelation illuminated the astral surroundings, portraying a vision of individuals attempting to bridge the gaps created by suspicion, seeking common ground amidst the encroaching darkness. In another anomaly, the group faced manifestations of defiance—an ominous future where the threads of fate remained entangled in resentment, alliances irreparably shattered by the weight of individual desperation. Symbols of revelation flickered with discordant energies, exposing the consequences of choices that resisted the call for reconciliation, leading to an irreversible fracture within the interconnected destinies. Guided by the guardian's echo, the group navigated through celestial challenges, confronting cosmic storms that mirrored the internal tempests of emotions. Symbols of revelation and interconnected destinies responded dynamically to their choices, showcasing the group's resilience but also the delicate balance they had to maintain in the face of the escalating desperation. In the heart of the celestial nexus, the group confronted a manifestation of the astral currents—a convergence where the threads of fate intersected with the consequences of shattered alliances. Symbols of revelation and interconnected destinies pulsed with a foreboding intensity, inviting the group to reflect on the ongoing narrative within the intricate dance of destinies influenced by their escalating struggles. With each reflection, the group grappled with the intensifying desperation, recognizing the precarious nature of their situation. The guardian's echo, a haunting cadence in the cosmic currents, urged them to confront the shadows within themselves and each other, to find a way forward amidst the encroaching darkness.

As they moved through the celestial nexus, symbols of revelation and interconnected destinies continued to guide their path. The astral currents pulsed with the energy of desperation, urging the group to explore further revelations in the dark and to discover the true extent of their collective resilience in the face of adversity. In the aftermath of the celestial nexus, the group felt the weight of desperation settling in, aware that the destiny of the interconnected individuals hung in the balance. The guardian's echo, now a somber companion through the trials of their own making, encouraged them to navigate the intricate expanse of the astral realms with newfound determination, seeking to weave a new chapter in the tapestry of their shared destiny—one shaped by resilience, unity, and the strength to overcome the encroaching desperation.

As the group pressed on through the astral realms, the guardian's echo continued to weave a narrative of uncertainty and tension. The celestial anomalies they encountered seemed to reflect the delicate dance between reconciliation and defiance, with the destiny of the group hanging in the balance. In one celestial anomaly, the group witnessed echoes of understanding—a potential future where the threads of fate, though strained, found a tentative equilibrium through shared experiences. Symbols of revelation illuminated the astral surroundings, portraying a vision of individuals striving to comprehend the motives behind suspicion, attempting to rebuild the bridges that had been weakened by desperation. In another anomaly, the group faced manifestations of resistance—an ominous future where the threads of fate remained entangled in unresolved conflicts, alliances irreparably shattered by the weight of individual desperation. Symbols of revelation flickered with discordant energies, exposing the consequences of choices that resisted the call for reconciliation, leading to an irreversible fracture within the interconnected destinies. Guided by the guardian's echo, the group navigated through celestial challenges, confronting cosmic storms that mirrored the internal tempests of emotions. Symbols of revelation and interconnected destinies responded dynamically to their choices, showcasing the group's resilience but also the delicate balance they had to maintain in the face of escalating desperation. In the heart of the celestial nexus, the group confronted a manifestation of the astral currents—a convergence where the threads of fate intersected with the consequences of shattered alliances. Symbols of revelation and interconnected destinies pulsed with a foreboding intensity, inviting the group to reflect on the ongoing narrative within the intricate dance of destinies influenced by their escalating struggles. With each reflection, the group grappled with the intensifying desperation, recognizing the precarious nature of their situation. The guardian's echo, a haunting cadence in the cosmic currents, urged them to confront the shadows within themselves and each other, to find a way forward amidst the encroaching darkness. As they moved through the celestial nexus, symbols of revelation and interconnected destinies continued to guide their path. The astral currents pulsed with the energy of desperation, urging the group to explore further revelations in the dark and to discover the true extent of their collective resilience in the face of adversity.

In the aftermath of the celestial nexus, the group felt the weight of desperation settling in, aware that the destiny of the interconnected individuals hung in the balance. The guardian's echo, now a somber companion through the trials of their own making, encouraged them to navigate the intricate expanse of the astral realms with newfound determination, seeking to weave a new chapter in the tapestry of their shared destiny—one shaped by resilience, unity, and the strength to overcome the encroaching desperation. The group, caught in the ebb and flow of the astral realms, found themselves navigating a delicate balance between understanding and resistance. The celestial anomalies painted glimpses of potential futures where the threads of fate either found a fragile equilibrium or remained ensnared in the web of irreparable conflicts.

In one celestial anomaly, the group confronted echoes of cooperation—a potential future where the threads of fate, though frayed, showed signs of repair through collaborative efforts. Symbols of revelation illuminated the astral surroundings, portraying a vision of individuals setting aside mistrust, striving to understand one another, and rebuilding the foundations of their alliances. In another anomaly, the group faced manifestations of defiance—an ominous future where the threads of fate resisted reconciliation, entangled in unresolved conflicts. Symbols of revelation flickered with discordant energies, exposing the consequences of choices that fueled a persistent resistance, leading to an irreversible fracture within the interconnected destinies. Guided by the guardian's echo, the group pressed on through celestial challenges, confronting cosmic storms that mirrored the internal tempests of emotions. Symbols of revelation and interconnected destinies responded dynamically to their choices, showcasing the group's resilience but also the delicate balance they had to maintain in the face of escalating desperation.

In the heart of the celestial nexus, the group confronted a manifestation of the astral currents—a convergence where the threads of fate intersected with the consequences of shattered alliances. Symbols of revelation and interconnected destinies pulsed with a foreboding intensity, inviting the group to reflect on the ongoing narrative within the intricate dance of destinies influenced by their escalating struggles. With each reflection, the group grappled with the intensifying desperation, recognizing the precarious nature of their situation. The guardian's echo, a haunting cadence in the cosmic currents, urged them to confront the shadows within themselves and each other, to find a way forward amidst the encroaching darkness. As they moved through the celestial nexus, symbols of revelation and interconnected destinies continued to guide their path. The astral currents pulsed with the energy of desperation, urging the group to explore further revelations in the dark and to discover the true extent of their collective resilience in the face of adversity. In the aftermath of the celestial nexus, the group felt the weight of desperation settling in, aware that the destiny of the interconnected individuals hung in the balance. The guardian's echo, now a somber companion through the trials of their own making, encouraged them to navigate the intricate expanse of the astral realms with newfound determination, seeking to weave a new chapter in the tapestry of their shared destiny—one shaped by resilience, unity, and the strength to overcome the encroaching desperation.

The group continued their journey through the astral realms, their destinies entwined in the delicate balance between cooperation and defiance. The celestial anomalies that unfolded before them presented diverging paths, each holding the promise of resolution or the peril of irreparable fractures. In one celestial anomaly, the group confronted echoes of empathy—a potential future where the threads of fate, though strained, demonstrated a collective effort to understand and support one another. Symbols of revelation illuminated the astral surroundings, portraying a vision of individuals setting aside differences, embracing vulnerability, and forging bonds anew in the face of desperation. In another anomaly, the group faced manifestations of obstinacy—an ominous future where the threads of fate resisted reconciliation, entangled in persistent conflicts. Symbols of revelation flickered with discordant energies, exposing the consequences of choices that fueled defiance, leading to an irreversible fracture within the interconnected destinies. Guided by the guardian's echo, the group traversed through celestial challenges, confronting cosmic storms that mirrored the internal tempests of emotions. Symbols of revelation and interconnected destinies responded dynamically to their choices, showcasing the group's resilience but also the fragile equilibrium they had to maintain in the face of escalating desperation. In the heart of the celestial nexus, the group confronted a manifestation of the astral currents—a convergence where the threads of fate intersected with the consequences of their choices. Symbols of revelation and interconnected destinies pulsed with a foreboding intensity, inviting the group to reflect on the ongoing narrative within the intricate dance of destinies influenced by their escalating struggles. With each reflection, the group grappled with the intensifying desperation, recognizing the precarious nature of their situation. The guardian's echo, a haunting cadence in the cosmic currents, urged them to confront the shadows within themselves and each other, to find a way forward amidst the encroaching darkness. As they moved through the celestial nexus, symbols of revelation and interconnected destinies continued to guide their path. The astral currents pulsed with the energy of desperation, urging the group to explore further revelations in the dark and to discover the true extent of their collective resilience in the face of adversity. In the aftermath of the celestial nexus, the group felt the weight of desperation settling in, aware that the destiny of the interconnected individuals hung in the balance. The guardian's echo, now a somber companion through the trials of their own making, encouraged them to navigate the intricate expanse of the astral realms with newfound determination, seeking to weave a new chapter in the tapestry of their shared destiny—one shaped by resilience, unity, and the strength to overcome the encroaching desperation.

The group moved forward, the celestial anomalies presenting glimpses of potential futures where the threads of fate wavered between cooperation and defiance. The astral currents carried them through an ethereal dance, echoing the internal struggles of the individuals as they sought a resolution to the growing desperation. In one celestial anomaly, the group witnessed echoes of reconciliation—a potential future where the threads of fate, though strained, showed signs of repair through shared understanding and empathy. Symbols of revelation illuminated the astral surroundings, portraying a vision of individuals setting aside mistrust, working collectively to mend the bonds that had been frayed by desperation. In another anomaly, the group faced manifestations of obstinacy—an ominous future where the threads of fate resisted reconciliation, entangled in persistent conflicts. Symbols of revelation flickered with discordant energies, exposing the consequences of choices that fueled defiance, leading to an irreversible fracture within the interconnected destinies. Guided by the guardian's echo, the group continued to navigate celestial challenges, confronting cosmic storms that mirrored the internal tempests of emotions. Symbols of revelation and interconnected destinies responded dynamically to their choices, showcasing the group's resilience but also the delicate equilibrium they had to maintain in the face of escalating desperation. In the heart of the celestial nexus, the group confronted a manifestation of the astral currents—a convergence where the threads of fate intersected with the consequences of their choices. Symbols of revelation and interconnected destinies pulsed with a foreboding intensity, inviting the group to reflect on the ongoing narrative within the intricate dance of destinies influenced by their escalating struggles. With each reflection, the group grappled with the intensifying desperation, recognizing the precarious nature of their situation. The guardian's echo, a haunting cadence in the cosmic currents, urged them to confront the shadows within themselves and each other, to find a way forward amidst the encroaching darkness.

As they moved through the celestial nexus, symbols of revelation and interconnected destinies continued to guide their path. The astral currents pulsed with the energy of desperation, urging the group to explore further revelations in the dark and to discover the true extent of their collective resilience in the face of adversity. In the aftermath of the celestial nexus, the group felt the weight of desperation settling in, aware that the destiny of the interconnected individuals hung in the balance. The guardian's echo, now a somber companion through the trials of their own making, encouraged them to navigate the intricate expanse of the astral realms with newfound determination, seeking to weave a new chapter in the tapestry of their shared destiny—one shaped by resilience, unity, and the strength to overcome the encroaching desperation. And so, with the echoes of reconciliation and obstinacy resonating in the cosmic currents, the group pressed on into the continuing cosmic tapestry, each step a testament to their resolve and the evolving nature of the interconnected destinies in the face of escalating desperation.

# Chapter 15: Echoes of the Past

The group, burdened by the weight of escalating desperation, continued their journey through the astral realms. As they ventured deeper, the celestial anomalies began to resonate with echoes from the past, intertwining the history of the individuals with the challenges of the present. In one celestial anomaly, the group confronted echoes of camaraderie—a vision of the past where the threads of fate were woven with shared laughter, trust, and shared experiences. Symbols of revelation illuminated the astral surroundings, portraying a time when the bonds among the individuals were unbreakable, untouched by the shadows that now threatened to engulf them. In another anomaly, the group faced manifestations of regret—an ominous reflection of choices made in the past that echoed into the present. Symbols of revelation flickered with regretful energies, exposing the consequences of actions that had sown the seeds of discord, contributing to the desperation that now gripped the interconnected destinies. Guided by the guardian's echo, the group traversed through these celestial echoes, confronting the ghosts of their past and the shadows that lurked within. Symbols of revelation and interconnected destinies responded dynamically to their choices, weaving a narrative that connected the echoes of the past with the challenges of the present. In the heart of the celestial nexus, the group confronted a manifestation of the astral currents—a convergence where the threads of fate intersected with the echoes of their shared history. Symbols of revelation and interconnected destinies pulsed with a haunting resonance, inviting the group to delve into the memories that shaped their present reality. With each reflection, the group grappled with the echoes of the past, recognizing how the decisions made in bygone moments reverberated into their current struggles. The guardian's echo, a melancholic cadence in the cosmic currents, urged them to confront the unresolved issues that lingered, to find a way to reconcile the echoes of the past with the challenges of the present. As they moved through the celestial nexus, symbols of revelation and interconnected destinies continued to guide their path. The astral currents pulsed with the energy of introspection, urging the group to explore further revelations in the echoes of the past and to discover the true extent of their collective resilience in the face of adversity. As the group delved deeper into the echoes of the past within the astral realms, the guardian's haunting melody served as a guide through the labyrinth of memories. The celestial anomalies unfolded like chapters from a forgotten book, revealing moments of unity and discord that had shaped the intertwined destinies.

In one celestial anomaly, the group confronted echoes of sacrifice—a poignant reminder of selflessness and cooperation in the face of adversity. Symbols of revelation illuminated the astral surroundings, portraying a time when the individuals had set aside personal interests for the greater good, laying the foundation for the unbreakable bonds that once defined them. In another anomaly, the group faced manifestations of betrayal—an ominous reflection of past transgressions that still cast shadows on their present struggles. Symbols of revelation flickered with the remnants of trust that had been shattered, exposing the consequences of actions that had sown seeds of discord, contributing to the desperation that now gripped the interconnected destinies. Guided by the guardian's echo, the group traversed through these celestial echoes, confronting the ghosts of their past and the shadows that lurked within. Symbols of revelation and interconnected destinies responded dynamically to their choices, weaving a narrative that connected the echoes of the past with the challenges of the present. In the heart of the celestial nexus, the group confronted a manifestation of the astral currents—a convergence where the threads of fate intersected with the echoes of their shared history. Symbols of revelation and interconnected destinies pulsed with a haunting resonance, inviting the group to delve into the memories that shaped their present reality. With each reflection, the group grappled with the echoes of the past, recognizing how the decisions made in bygone moments reverberated into their current struggles. The guardian's echo, a melancholic cadence in the cosmic currents, urged them to confront the unresolved issues that lingered, to find a way to reconcile the echoes of the past with the challenges of the present. As they moved through the celestial nexus, symbols of revelation and interconnected destinies continued to guide their path. The astral currents pulsed with the energy of introspection, urging the group to explore further revelations in the echoes of the past and to discover the true extent of their collective resilience in the face of adversity.

In the aftermath of the celestial nexus, the group felt a profound connection to the echoes of the past, realizing that understanding their shared history was key to navigating the challenges ahead. The guardian's echo, now a guide through the tapestry of memories, encouraged them to unravel the threads of the past, seeking to weave a new chapter in the interconnected destinies—one shaped by reflection, reconciliation, and the strength to face the echoes of desperation that still lingered. The group, entwined in the echoes of their past, pressed forward through the astral realms, guided by the poignant melody of the guardian's echo. Each celestial anomaly revealed a different facet of their shared history, offering both moments of unity and the lingering shadows of discord.

In one celestial anomaly, the group confronted echoes of resilience—a vision of the past where the threads of fate demonstrated the strength to withstand adversity. Symbols of revelation illuminated the astral surroundings, portraying a time when the individuals had faced challenges head-on, forging a path through hardships and strengthening their bonds in the process. In another anomaly, the group faced manifestations of remorse—an ominous reflection of actions that had left scars on their collective history. Symbols of revelation flickered with regretful energies, exposing the consequences of choices that had strained the interconnected destinies, contributing to the desperation that now held them in its grip. Guided by the guardian's echo, the group traversed through these celestial echoes, confronting the ghosts of their past and the shadows that lingered within. Symbols of revelation and interconnected destinies responded dynamically to their choices, weaving a narrative that connected the echoes of the past with the challenges of the present. In the heart of the celestial nexus, the group confronted a manifestation of the astral currents—a convergence where the threads of fate intersected with the echoes of their shared history. Symbols of revelation and interconnected destinies pulsed with a haunting resonance, inviting the group to delve deeper into the memories that shaped their present reality. With each reflection, the group grappled with the echoes of resilience and remorse, recognizing how the decisions made in bygone moments reverberated into their current struggles. The guardian's echo, a melancholic cadence in the cosmic currents, urged them to confront the unresolved issues that lingered, to find a way to reconcile the echoes of the past with the challenges of the present. As they moved through the celestial nexus, symbols of revelation and interconnected destinies continued to guide their path. The astral currents pulsed with the energy of introspection, urging the group to explore further revelations in the echoes of the past and to discover the true extent of their collective resilience in the face of adversity.

In the aftermath of the celestial nexus, the group felt a profound connection to the echoes of the past, realizing that understanding their shared history was key to navigating the challenges ahead. The guardian's echo, now a guide through the tapestry of memories, encouraged them to unravel the threads of the past, seeking to weave a new chapter in the interconnected destinies—one shaped by reflection, reconciliation, and the strength to face the echoes of desperation that still lingered.

As the group continued their journey through the astral realms, the echoes of resilience and remorse reverberated through the cosmic tapestry of their shared history. The guardian's haunting melody persisted, guiding them through celestial anomalies that unraveled the threads of their past. In one celestial anomaly, the group confronted echoes of reconciliation—a vision of the past where the threads of fate demonstrated the potential for healing and forgiveness. Symbols of revelation illuminated the astral surroundings, portraying a time when individuals had set aside grievances, allowing the wounds of the past to mend and fostering a renewed sense of unity. In another anomaly, the group faced manifestations of lingering conflict—an ominous reflection of unresolved tensions that continued to cast shadows over their shared history. Symbols of revelation flickered with discordant energies, exposing the consequences of choices that had perpetuated a cycle of strife, contributing to the desperation that now gripped the interconnected destinies. Guided by the guardian's echo, the group traversed through these celestial echoes, confronting the ghosts of their past and the shadows that lingered within. Symbols of revelation and interconnected destinies responded dynamically to their choices, weaving a narrative that connected the echoes of the past with the challenges of the present.

In the heart of the celestial nexus, the group confronted a manifestation of the astral currents—a convergence where the threads of fate intersected with the echoes of their shared history. Symbols of revelation and interconnected destinies pulsed with a haunting resonance, inviting the group to delve even deeper into the memories that shaped their present reality. With each reflection, the group grappled with the echoes of reconciliation and lingering conflict, recognizing how the decisions made in bygone moments reverberated into their current struggles. The guardian's echo, a melancholic cadence in the cosmic currents, urged them to confront the unresolved issues that lingered, to find a way to reconcile the echoes of the past with the challenges of the present. As they moved through the celestial nexus, symbols of revelation and interconnected destinies continued to guide their path. The astral currents pulsed with the energy of introspection, urging the group to explore further revelations in the echoes of the past and to discover the true extent of their collective resilience in the face of adversity. In the aftermath of the celestial nexus, the group felt a profound connection to the echoes of the past, realizing that understanding their shared history was key to navigating the challenges ahead. The guardian's echo, now a guide through the tapestry of memories, encouraged them to unravel the threads of the past, seeking to weave a new chapter in the interconnected destinies—one shaped by reflection, reconciliation, and the strength to face the echoes of desperation that still lingered.

The group, attuned to the echoes of reconciliation and lingering conflict within the astral realms, pressed forward into the cosmic tapestry that wove together their shared history. The guardian's ethereal melody guided them through the celestial anomalies, each revealing a different facet of their intertwined destinies. In one celestial anomaly, the group confronted echoes of forgiveness—a vision of the past where the threads of fate demonstrated the transformative power of letting go. Symbols of revelation illuminated the astral surroundings, portraying a time when individuals, burdened by past grievances, found a way to release the shackles of resentment and embrace a renewed sense of understanding. In another anomaly, the group faced manifestations of persistent discord—an ominous reflection of unresolved tensions that continued to cast shadows over their shared history. Symbols of revelation flickered with discordant energies, exposing the consequences of choices that had perpetuated a cycle of strife, contributing to the desperation that now gripped the interconnected destinies. Guided by the guardian's echo, the group traversed through these celestial echoes, confronting the ghosts of their past and the shadows that lingered within. Symbols of revelation and interconnected destinies responded dynamically to their choices, weaving a narrative that connected the echoes of the past with the challenges of the present. In the heart of the celestial nexus, the group confronted a manifestation of the astral currents—a convergence where the threads of fate intersected with the echoes of their shared history. Symbols of revelation and interconnected destinies pulsed with a haunting resonance, inviting the group to delve even deeper into the memories that shaped their present reality. With each reflection, the group grappled with the echoes of forgiveness and persistent discord, recognizing how the decisions made in bygone moments reverberated into their current struggles. The guardian's echo, a melancholic cadence in the cosmic currents, urged them to confront the unresolved issues that lingered, to find a way to reconcile the echoes of the past with the challenges of the present.

As they moved through the celestial nexus, symbols of revelation and interconnected destinies continued to guide their path. The astral currents pulsed with the energy of introspection, urging the group to explore further revelations in the echoes of the past and to discover the true extent of their collective resilience in the face of adversity. In the aftermath of the celestial nexus, the group felt a profound connection to the echoes of the past, realizing that understanding their shared history was key to navigating the challenges ahead. The guardian's echo, now a guide through the tapestry of memories, encouraged them to unravel the threads of the past, seeking to weave a new chapter in the interconnected destinies—one shaped by reflection, reconciliation, and the strength to face the echoes of desperation that still lingered.

The group, enveloped in the celestial echoes of forgiveness and persistent discord, journeyed deeper into the astral realms. The guardian's haunting melody resonated, guiding them through the cosmic tapestry that unraveled the complexities of their shared history. In one celestial anomaly, the group confronted echoes of understanding—a vision of the past where the threads of fate demonstrated the power of empathy and compassion. Symbols of revelation illuminated the astral surroundings, portraying a time when individuals, faced with adversities, sought to comprehend the perspectives of others, fostering a spirit of unity that transcended their differences. In another anomaly, the group faced manifestations of unyielding strife—an ominous reflection of enduring conflicts that cast a long shadow over their collective history. Symbols of revelation flickered with discordant energies, exposing the consequences of choices that perpetuated a cycle of disagreement, contributing to the desperation that now gripped the interconnected destinies. Guided by the guardian's echo, the group traversed through these celestial echoes, confronting the ghosts of their past and the shadows that lingered within. Symbols of revelation and interconnected destinies responded dynamically to their choices, weaving a narrative that connected the echoes of the past with the challenges of the present. In the heart of the celestial nexus, the group confronted a manifestation of the astral currents—a convergence where the threads of fate intersected with the echoes of their shared history. Symbols of revelation and interconnected destinies pulsed with a haunting resonance, inviting the group to delve even deeper into the memories that shaped their present reality. With each reflection, the group grappled with the echoes of understanding and unyielding strife, recognizing how the decisions made in bygone moments reverberated into their current struggles. The guardian's echo, a melancholic cadence in the cosmic currents, urged them to confront the unresolved issues that lingered, to find a way to reconcile the echoes of the past with the challenges of the present.

As they moved through the celestial nexus, symbols of revelation and interconnected destinies continued to guide their path. The astral currents pulsed with the energy of introspection, urging the group to explore further revelations in the echoes of the past and to discover the true extent of their collective resilience in the face of adversity. In the aftermath of the celestial nexus, the group felt a profound connection to the echoes of the past, realizing that understanding their shared history was key to navigating the challenges ahead. The guardian's echo, now a guide through the tapestry of memories, encouraged them to unravel the threads of the past, seeking to weave a new chapter in the interconnected destinies—one shaped by reflection, reconciliation, and the strength to face the echoes of desperation that still lingered.

The group, immersed in the celestial echoes of understanding and unyielding strife, advanced through the astral realms guided by the haunting melody of the guardian's echo. Each celestial anomaly unfolded a chapter of their shared history, revealing the intricate threads of connection and discord that had shaped their destinies. In one celestial anomaly, the group confronted echoes of unity—a vision of the past where the threads of fate demonstrated the strength found in collaboration. Symbols of revelation illuminated the astral surroundings, portraying a time when individuals, amidst challenges, forged alliances and worked together to overcome adversity, laying the foundation for an enduring bond. In another anomaly, the group faced manifestations of enduring conflict—an ominous reflection of persistent tensions that cast shadows over their collective history. Symbols of revelation flickered with discordant energies, exposing the consequences of choices that had perpetuated a cycle of disagreement, contributing to the desperation that now gripped the interconnected destinies.

Guided by the guardian's echo, the group traversed through these celestial echoes, confronting the ghosts of their past and the shadows that lingered within. Symbols of revelation and interconnected destinies responded dynamically to their choices, weaving a narrative that connected the echoes of the past with the challenges of the present. In the heart of the celestial nexus, the group confronted a manifestation of the astral currents—a convergence where the threads of fate intersected with the echoes of their shared history. Symbols of revelation and interconnected destinies pulsed with a haunting resonance, inviting the group to delve even deeper into the memories that shaped their present reality. With each reflection, the group grappled with the echoes of unity and enduring conflict, recognizing how the decisions made in bygone moments reverberated into their current struggles. The guardian's echo, a melancholic cadence in the cosmic currents, urged them to confront the unresolved issues that lingered, to find a way to reconcile the echoes of the past with the challenges of the present. As they moved through the celestial nexus, symbols of revelation and interconnected destinies continued to guide their path. The astral currents pulsed with the energy of introspection, urging the group to explore further revelations in the echoes of the past and to discover the true extent of their collective resilience in the face of adversity. In the aftermath of the celestial nexus, the group felt a profound connection to the echoes of the past, realizing that understanding their shared history was key to navigating the challenges ahead. The guardian's echo, now a guide through the tapestry of memories, encouraged them to unravel the threads of the past, seeking to weave a new chapter in the interconnected destinies—one shaped by reflection, reconciliation, and the strength to face the echoes of desperation that still lingered.

The group, surrounded by the echoes of unity and enduring conflict, forged ahead in the astral realms, guided by the haunting melody of the guardian's echo. The celestial anomalies continued to unfold, revealing the intricate layers of their shared history and the challenges that had shaped their destinies. In one celestial anomaly, the group confronted echoes of cooperation—a vision of the past where the threads of fate showcased the power of individuals coming together. Symbols of revelation illuminated the astral surroundings, portraying a time when trust and collaboration had triumphed over adversity, leading to moments of shared victory and resilience. In another anomaly, the group faced manifestations of lingering discord—an ominous reflection of unresolved tensions that cast shadows over their collective history. Symbols of revelation flickered with discordant energies, exposing the consequences of choices that had perpetuated a cycle of disagreement, contributing to the desperation that now gripped the interconnected destinies. Guided by the guardian's echo, the group traversed through these celestial echoes, confronting the ghosts of their past and the shadows that lingered within. Symbols of revelation and interconnected destinies responded dynamically to their choices, weaving a narrative that connected the echoes of the past with the challenges of the present. In the heart of the celestial nexus, the group confronted a manifestation of the astral currents—a convergence where the threads of fate intersected with the echoes of their shared history. Symbols of revelation and interconnected destinies pulsed with a haunting resonance, inviting the group to delve even deeper into the memories that shaped their present reality.

With each reflection, the group grappled with the echoes of cooperation and lingering discord, recognizing how the decisions made in bygone moments reverberated into their current struggles. The guardian's echo, a melancholic cadence in the cosmic currents, urged them to confront the unresolved issues that lingered, to find a way to reconcile the echoes of the past with the challenges of the present. As they moved through the celestial nexus, symbols of revelation and interconnected destinies continued to guide their path. The astral currents pulsed with the energy of introspection, urging the group to explore further revelations in the echoes of the past and to discover the true extent of their collective resilience in the face of adversity. In the aftermath of the celestial nexus, the group felt a profound connection to the echoes of the past, realizing that understanding their shared history was key to navigating the challenges ahead. The guardian's echo, now a guide through the tapestry of memories, encouraged them to unravel the threads of the past, seeking to weave a new chapter in the interconnected destinies—one shaped by reflection, reconciliation, and the strength to face the echoes of desperation that still lingered.

# Chapter 16: Darkness Descends

The astral realms stretched out before the group, a cosmic canvas painted with the echoes of their shared history. The guardian's haunting melody lingered in the air as they entered a new celestial anomaly, where the threads of fate intertwined with the whispers of redemption. In this celestial anomaly, the group confronted echoes of transformation—a vision of the past where the threads of fate demonstrated the potential for change and growth. Symbols of revelation illuminated the astral surroundings, portraying a time when individuals, facing their flaws and mistakes, embarked on a journey of redemption, seeking to mend the fractures that had threatened to shatter their unity. As the group moved through this astral realm, the guardian's echo resonated with a hopeful cadence, urging them to explore the possibilities of redemption within the tapestry of their interconnected destinies. Symbols of revelation and interconnected destinies responded dynamically to their choices, weaving a narrative that connected the echoes of transformation with the challenges of the present. In the heart of the celestial nexus, the group confronted a manifestation of the astral currents—a convergence where the threads of fate intersected with the whispers of redemption. Symbols of revelation and interconnected destinies pulsed with a rejuvenating energy, inviting the group to delve even deeper into the transformative moments that shaped their present reality. With each reflection, the group grappled with the echoes of redemption, recognizing the power of forgiveness and personal growth in the face of past mistakes. The guardian's echo, a guiding melody in the cosmic currents, encouraged them to embrace the potential for change and to navigate the intricacies of redemption with sincerity and humility.

As they moved through the celestial nexus, symbols of revelation and interconnected destinies continued to guide their path. The astral currents pulsed with the energy of renewal, urging the group to explore further revelations in the whispers of redemption and to discover the true extent of their collective resilience in the face of adversity. In the ongoing tapestry of destinies, the group felt a profound connection to the echoes of transformation and redemption, realizing that the journey toward unity and survival required acknowledging and rectifying the mistakes of the past. The guardian's echo, now a beacon of hope through the tapestry of memories, encouraged them to embrace the whispers of redemption, seeking to weave a new chapter in the interconnected destinies—one shaped by reflection, transformation, and the strength to face the echoes of desperation that still lingered. The astral realms stretched out before the group, a cosmic canvas painted with the echoes of their shared history. The guardian's haunting melody lingered in the air as they entered a new celestial anomaly, where the threads of fate intertwined with the whispers of redemption. In this celestial anomaly, the group confronted echoes of transformation—a vision of the past where the threads of fate demonstrated the potential for change and growth. Symbols of revelation illuminated the astral surroundings, portraying a time when individuals, facing their flaws and mistakes, embarked on a journey of redemption, seeking to mend the fractures that had threatened to shatter their unity. As the group moved through this astral realm, the guardian's echo resonated with a hopeful cadence, urging them to explore the possibilities of redemption within the tapestry of their interconnected destinies. Symbols of revelation and interconnected destinies responded dynamically to their choices, weaving a narrative that connected the echoes of transformation with the challenges of the present.

In the heart of the celestial nexus, the group confronted a manifestation of the astral currents—a convergence where the threads of fate intersected with the whispers of redemption. Symbols of revelation and interconnected destinies pulsed with a rejuvenating energy, inviting the group to delve even deeper into the transformative moments that shaped their present reality. With each reflection, the group grappled with the echoes of redemption, recognizing the power of forgiveness and personal growth in the face of past mistakes. The guardian's echo, a guiding melody in the cosmic currents, encouraged them to embrace the potential for change and to navigate the intricacies of redemption with sincerity and humility. As they moved through the celestial nexus, symbols of revelation and interconnected destinies continued to guide their path. The astral currents pulsed with the energy of renewal, urging the group to explore further revelations in the whispers of redemption and to discover the true extent of their collective resilience in the face of adversity. In the ongoing tapestry of destinies, the group felt a profound connection to the echoes of transformation and redemption, realizing that the journey toward unity and survival required acknowledging and rectifying the mistakes of the past. The guardian's echo, now a beacon of hope through the tapestry of memories, encouraged them to embrace the whispers of redemption, seeking to weave a new chapter in the interconnected destinies—one shaped by reflection, transformation, and the strength to face the echoes of desperation that still lingered. The group, fueled by the whispers of redemption, moved forward into the ever-shifting astral realms. The celestial anomalies unfolded like chapters of a cosmic epic, revealing new layers of their intertwined destinies. The guardian's echo continued to guide them, now accompanied by a subtle undertone of anticipation.

In this new celestial anomaly, the group confronted echoes of shadows—a vision of the past where the threads of fate intertwined with the hidden aspects of their shared history. Symbols of revelation dimmed, casting an enigmatic ambiance as the astral surroundings portrayed moments when secrets and concealed truths threatened to fracture the unity that had once bound them together. As the group ventured deeper into this astral realm, the guardian's echo took on a cautionary tone, urging them to navigate the veiled secrets with care. Symbols of revelation and interconnected destinies responded dynamically to their choices, weaving a narrative that connected the echoes of shadows with the challenges of the present. In the heart of the celestial nexus, the group confronted a manifestation of the astral currents—a convergence where the threads of fate intersected with the veiled shadows. Symbols of revelation and interconnected destinies pulsed with a mysterious energy, inviting the group to unravel the hidden truths that had woven themselves into the fabric of their interconnected destinies. With each reflection, the group grappled with the echoes of shadows, recognizing the importance of transparency and trust in overcoming the challenges that lay ahead. The guardian's echo, a vigilant melody in the cosmic currents, cautioned them to face the concealed aspects of their history with courage and honesty. As they moved through the celestial nexus, symbols of revelation and interconnected destinies continued to guide their path. The astral currents pulsed with the energy of introspection, urging the group to delve into the shadows and unveil the truths that could shape their journey toward survival.

In the aftermath of the celestial nexus, the group felt a heightened awareness of the echoes of shadows, realizing that confronting the veiled aspects of their shared history was essential for forging a path forward. The guardian's echo, now a watchful guide through the tapestry of memories, encouraged them to unravel the hidden threads, seeking to weave a new chapter in the interconnected destinies—one marked by transparency, understanding, and the strength to face the echoes of desperation that still lingered. The group, emboldened by their resolve to uncover the veiled shadows within their shared history, journeyed through the astral realms. The celestial anomalies continued to unfold, revealing a tapestry woven with the threads of secrecy and the unspoken truths that had shaped their destinies. In this celestial anomaly, the group confronted echoes of revelation—a vision of the past where the threads of fate intertwined with the moments of clarity that had the power to dispel the shadows. Symbols of revelation burned brightly, piercing through the astral surroundings, portraying a time when hidden truths were exposed, and the group faced the consequences of their concealed actions. As they navigated this astral realm, the guardian's echo resonated with a tone of introspection, urging the group to confront the revelations with courage and understanding. Symbols of revelation and interconnected destinies responded dynamically to their choices, weaving a narrative that connected the echoes of revelation with the challenges of the present.

In the heart of the celestial nexus, the group confronted a manifestation of the astral currents—a convergence where the threads of fate intersected with the embers of revelation. Symbols of revelation and interconnected destinies pulsed with an illuminating energy, inviting the group to delve even deeper into the truths that had long been obscured. With each reflection, the group grappled with the echoes of revelation, recognizing the transformative power that honesty and transparency held. The guardian's echo, a guiding melody in the cosmic currents, encouraged them to embrace the clarity that came with acknowledging the concealed aspects of their history. As they moved through the celestial nexus, symbols of revelation and interconnected destinies continued to guide their path. The astral currents pulsed with the energy of enlightenment, urging the group to explore further revelations and to discover the true extent of their collective resilience in the face of adversity. In the aftermath of the celestial nexus, the group felt a profound weight lifted from their intertwined destinies. The echoes of revelation lingered, marking a turning point in their journey. The guardian's echo, now a beacon of insight through the tapestry of memories, encouraged them to carry the lessons learned forward, seeking to weave a new chapter—one marked by transparency, understanding, and the strength to face the echoes of desperation that still lingered. As the group ventured further into the astral realms, the echoes of revelation lingered, casting a newfound light upon their shared history. The celestial anomalies continued to unfold, revealing a complex interplay of trust and mistrust within the intricate threads of fate. In this celestial anomaly, the group confronted echoes of trust—a vision of the past where the threads of fate interwoven with moments of genuine connection and reliance. Symbols of revelation illuminated the astral surroundings, portraying a time when individuals, stripped of secrets, began to rebuild the foundations of trust that had once bound them together. Guided by the guardian's echo, the group moved through this astral realm with a sense of hope and vulnerability. Symbols of revelation and interconnected destinies responded dynamically to their choices, weaving a narrative that connected the echoes of trust with the challenges of the present. In the heart of the celestial nexus, the group confronted a manifestation of the astral currents—a convergence where the threads of fate intersected with the fragile whispers of trust. Symbols of revelation and interconnected destinies pulsed with a delicate energy, inviting the group to delve even deeper into the bonds that could mend the fractures within their interconnected destinies.

With each reflection, the group grappled with the echoes of trust, recognizing the significance of rebuilding and nurturing the connections that had been strained by the shadows of secrecy. The guardian's echo, a reassuring melody in the cosmic currents, encouraged them to embrace the vulnerability that came with trust, acknowledging that it was a crucial foundation for overcoming the challenges they faced. As they moved through the celestial nexus, symbols of revelation and interconnected destinies continued to guide their path. The astral currents pulsed with the energy of renewal, urging the group to explore the whispers of trust and to discover the true extent of their collective resilience in the face of adversity. In the aftermath of the celestial nexus, the group felt a subtle shift in the air—a soft breeze carrying the whispers of trust. The guardian's echo, now a companion through the tapestry of memories, encouraged them to nurture these fragile bonds, seeking to weave a new chapter in the interconnected destinies—one marked by trust, understanding, and the strength to face the echoes of desperation that still lingered.

The group, buoyed by the fragile whispers of trust, continued their journey through the astral realms. The celestial anomalies unfolded like chapters, each revealing a facet of their interconnected destinies. The guardian's echo, now a melody of reassurance, guided them through a cosmic dance where unity and division wove themselves into the fabric of their shared history. In this celestial anomaly, the group confronted echoes of unity—a vision of the past where the threads of fate intricately entwined with moments of collective strength and cooperation. Symbols of revelation shone brightly, illuminating the astral surroundings and depicting a time when individuals, bound by trust and transparency, stood together to face adversity. Guided by the guardian's echo, the group navigated this astral realm with a renewed sense of purpose. Symbols of revelation and interconnected destinies responded dynamically to their choices, weaving a narrative that connected the echoes of unity with the challenges of the present. In the heart of the celestial nexus, the group confronted a manifestation of the astral currents—a convergence where the threads of fate intersected with the resonance of unity. Symbols of revelation and interconnected destinies pulsed with a harmonious energy, inviting the group to delve even deeper into the essence of their collective strength. With each reflection, the group embraced the echoes of unity, recognizing the power that came from standing together, transparent and trusting. The guardian's echo, a harmonizing melody in the cosmic currents, encouraged them to cultivate a sense of solidarity, understanding that true unity required ongoing commitment and the strength to weather the storms that lay ahead.

As they moved through the celestial nexus, symbols of revelation and interconnected destinies continued to guide their path. The astral currents pulsed with the energy of togetherness, urging the group to explore further the resonance of unity and to discover the true extent of their collective resilience in the face of adversity. In the aftermath of the celestial nexus, the group felt a deep connection to the echoes of unity, realizing that their shared strength was the key to overcoming the challenges ahead. The guardian's echo, now a conductor through the tapestry of memories, encouraged them to nurture this unity, seeking to weave a new chapter in the interconnected destinies—one marked by solidarity, understanding, and the strength to face the echoes of desperation that still lingered. With the resonance of unity echoing in the cosmic currents, the group pressed on into the continuing cosmic tapestry, each step a testament to their commitment to standing together and the evolving nature of their interconnected destinies in the face of escalating desperation and the promise that unity held for their shared future.

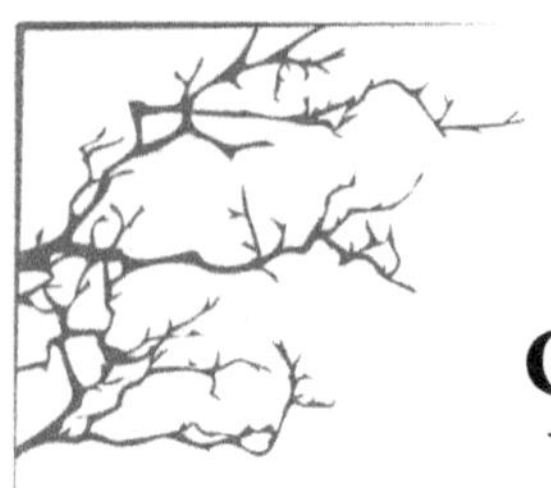

# Chapter 17: The Breaking Point

The group, now bound by fragile trust and resonating unity, traversed deeper into the astral realms. The celestial anomalies took on a foreboding aura, as the threads of fate unraveled a chapter laden with tension and trials. The guardian's echo, once reassuring, now carried an undertone of apprehension. In this celestial anomaly, the group confronted echoes of discord—a vision of the past where the threads of fate interwoven with moments of tension and strain. Symbols of revelation flickered with an ominous glow, illuminating the astral surroundings and portraying a time when the bonds of unity were tested, threatening to snap under the weight of internal conflicts. Guided by the guardian's echo, the group navigated this astral realm with a heightened sense of awareness. Symbols of revelation and interconnected destinies responded dynamically to their choices, weaving a narrative that connected the echoes of discord with the challenges of the present. In the heart of the celestial nexus, the group confronted a manifestation of the astral currents—a convergence where the threads of fate intersected with the looming breaking point. Symbols of revelation and interconnected destinies pulsed with a discordant energy, inviting the group to delve even deeper into the fractures that threatened their hard-won unity. With each reflection, the group grappled with the echoes of discord, recognizing the fragile nature of their bonds and the need to address the unresolved tensions that simmered beneath the surface. The guardian's echo, a cautionary melody in the cosmic currents, urged them to face the looming breaking point with courage and a willingness to confront the challenges that lay ahead. As they moved through the celestial nexus, symbols of revelation and interconnected destinies continued to guide their path. The astral currents pulsed with the energy of confrontation, urging the group to explore the breaking point and to discover the true extent of their collective resilience in the face of internal strife.

In the aftermath of the celestial nexus, the group felt the weight of the echoes of discord pressing upon them, realizing that their unity was fragile and required constant vigilance. The guardian's echo, now a guide through the tense tapestry of memories, encouraged them to navigate the breaking point with open communication, seeking to weave a new chapter in the interconnected destinies—one marked by resolution, understanding, and the strength to face the echoes of desperation that still lingered. The group, now acutely aware of the echoes of discord within their interconnected destinies, forged ahead in the astral realms. The celestial anomalies unfolded like a turbulent storm, each thread of fate unraveling a moment that tested the bonds of unity they had fought so hard to rebuild. The guardian's echo, a somber melody, accompanied them through this turbulent journey. In this celestial anomaly, the group confronted echoes of confrontation—a vision of the past where the threads of fate intertwined with moments of disagreement and strife. Symbols of revelation glowed with an intense luminosity, casting stark shadows on the astral surroundings, portraying a time when unresolved tensions threatened to fracture the very fabric of their newfound unity. Guided by the guardian's echo, the group navigated this astral realm with a heavy heart. Symbols of revelation and interconnected destinies responded dynamically to their choices, weaving a narrative that connected the echoes of confrontation with the challenges of the present. In the heart of the celestial nexus, the group confronted a manifestation of the astral currents—a convergence where the threads of fate intersected with the fracture points. Symbols of revelation and interconnected destinies pulsed with a dissonant energy, inviting the group to delve even deeper into the fractures that threatened to tear them apart. With each reflection, the group grappled with the echoes of confrontation, recognizing that the breaking point was not a distant threat but a present reality. The guardian's echo, a mournful melody in the cosmic currents, urged them to confront the fractures head-on, to find resolutions and rebuild their bonds before it was too late. As they moved through the celestial nexus, symbols of revelation and interconnected destinies continued to guide their path. The astral currents pulsed with the energy of introspection, urging the group to explore the fracture points and to discover the true extent of their collective resilience in the face of internal strife.

In the aftermath of the celestial nexus, the group felt the strain of the fractures within their once-unbreakable bonds. The guardian's echo, now a companion through the tapestry of discordant memories, encouraged them to mend the fractures with open communication, seeking to weave a new chapter in the interconnected destinies—one marked by healing, understanding, and the strength to face the echoes of desperation that still lingered. The group, burdened by the fractures within their once-solid bonds, moved forward in the astral realms. The celestial anomalies unfolded like a delicate dance, each step revealing the intricacies of their interconnected destinies. The guardian's echo, now a melody of yearning, guided them through a landscape marked by tension and the echoes of discord. In this celestial anomaly, the group confronted echoes of solitude—a vision of the past where the threads of fate intertwined with moments of isolation and misunderstanding. Symbols of revelation cast a muted glow, illuminating the astral surroundings and portraying a time when individuals, grappling with internal conflicts, withdrew into their own emotional realms. Guided by the guardian's echo, the group navigated this astral realm with a renewed sense of empathy. Symbols of revelation and interconnected destinies responded dynamically to their choices, weaving a narrative that connected the echoes of solitude with the challenges of the present. In the heart of the celestial nexus, the group confronted a manifestation of the astral currents—a convergence where the threads of fate intersected with the lingering echoes of reconciliation. Symbols of revelation and interconnected destinies pulsed with a hopeful energy, inviting the group to delve even deeper into the emotional landscapes that had driven them apart. With each reflection, the group grappled with the echoes of solitude, recognizing the isolation that had crept into their once-unified front. The guardian's echo, a melancholic melody in the cosmic currents, urged them to seek reconciliation, to bridge the emotional gaps that threatened their collective strength.

As they moved through the celestial nexus, symbols of revelation and interconnected destinies continued to guide their path. The astral currents pulsed with the energy of understanding, urging the group to explore the echoes of reconciliation and to discover the true extent of their collective resilience in the face of internal strife. In the aftermath of the celestial nexus, the group felt a yearning for reconciliation, a shared desire to heal the wounds that had driven them apart. The guardian's echo, now a guide through the tapestry of emotional memories, encouraged them to embrace open communication, seeking to weave a new chapter in the interconnected destinies—one marked by understanding, reconciliation, and the strength to face the echoes of desperation that still lingered. The group, yearning for reconciliation, ventured deeper into the astral realms. The celestial anomalies unfolded with an air of delicate anticipation, each thread of fate weaving the story of their interconnected destinies. The guardian's echo, now a melody of tentative hope, guided them through a landscape marked by the echoes of solitude and the desire for understanding. In this celestial anomaly, the group confronted echoes of vulnerability—a vision of the past where the threads of fate intertwined with moments of raw honesty and emotional exposure. Symbols of revelation cast a gentle glow, illuminating the astral surroundings and portraying a time when individuals, shedding their defensive barriers, sought to bridge the emotional gaps that had driven wedges between them. Guided by the guardian's echo, the group navigated this astral realm with a shared commitment to vulnerability. Symbols of revelation and interconnected destinies responded dynamically to their choices, weaving a narrative that connected the echoes of vulnerability with the challenges of the present. In the heart of the celestial nexus, the group confronted a manifestation of the astral currents—a convergence where the threads of fate intersected with the fragile truce. Symbols of revelation and interconnected destinies pulsed with a cautious energy, inviting the group to delve even deeper into the emotional landscapes that had driven them apart, now with a shared commitment to understanding. With each reflection, the group embraced the echoes of vulnerability, recognizing the strength that came from exposing their true selves and understanding the emotions that had fueled the fractures. The guardian's echo, a tender melody in the cosmic currents, urged them to tread carefully, nurturing the fragile truce that had begun to take shape.

As they moved through the celestial nexus, symbols of revelation and interconnected destinies continued to guide their path. The astral currents pulsed with the energy of reconciliation, urging the group to explore further the delicate truce and to discover the true extent of their collective resilience in the face of internal strife. In the aftermath of the celestial nexus, the group felt the weight of the fragile truce, realizing that the path to true reconciliation required patience and ongoing effort. The guardian's echo, now a companion through the tapestry of emotional memories, encouraged them to build upon the fragile truce, seeking to weave a new chapter in the interconnected destinies—one marked by mutual understanding, shared vulnerability, and the strength to face the echoes of desperation that still lingered. Guided by the melody of the guardian's echo, the group continued to traverse the astral realms, navigating the delicate truce that hung in the balance. The celestial anomalies unfolded with a mix of tension and anticipation, each moment etching a fragment of their shared history. The guardian's echo, now a harmonious blend of hope and caution, accompanied them through a landscape fraught with the echoes of vulnerability and the persistent yearning for resolution. In this celestial anomaly, the group confronted echoes of introspection—a vision of the past where the threads of fate intertwined with moments of deep self-reflection. Symbols of revelation cast a thoughtful glow, illuminating the astral surroundings and portraying a time when individuals, moved by the fragile truce, began to explore the roots of their internal conflicts and seek resolution within themselves. Guided by the guardian's echo, the group navigated this astral realm with a shared commitment to introspection. Symbols of revelation and interconnected destinies responded dynamically to their choices, weaving a narrative that connected the echoes of vulnerability with the challenges of the present.

In the heart of the celestial nexus, the group confronted a manifestation of the astral currents—a convergence where the threads of fate intersected with the echoing resolution. Symbols of revelation and interconnected destinies pulsed with a thoughtful energy, inviting the group to delve even deeper into the introspective journey that held the key to lasting harmony. With each reflection, the group embraced the echoes of vulnerability and introspection, recognizing that true resolution required understanding the intricacies of their individual selves. The guardian's echo, a wise melody in the cosmic currents, urged them to continue their journey of self-discovery, emphasizing that internal harmony would fortify the delicate truce that bound them together. As they moved through the celestial nexus, symbols of revelation and interconnected destinies continued to guide their path. The astral currents pulsed with the energy of contemplation, urging the group to explore further the echoing resolution and to discover the true extent of their collective resilience in the face of internal strife. In the aftermath of the celestial nexus, the group felt a sense of internal clarity, realizing that the echoes of vulnerability and introspection were the pillars supporting the fragile truce. The guardian's echo, now a guide through the tapestry of self-discovery, encouraged them to continue their introspective journey, seeking to weave a new chapter in the interconnected destinies—one marked by internal harmony, mutual understanding, and the strength to face the echoes of desperation that still lingered.

# Chapter 18: From Ashes to Resolve

As the group continued their journey through the astral realms, a peculiar stillness settled in the cosmic currents. The celestial anomalies unfolded with an eerie calm, each thread of fate hanging in suspense. The guardian's echo, now a silent undertone, accompanied them through a landscape marked by the echoes of vulnerability, introspection, and the delicate truce that held their collective destinies in a precarious balance. In this celestial anomaly, the group confronted echoes of serenity—a vision of the past where the threads of fate intertwined with moments of quiet contemplation and silent understanding. Symbols of revelation cast a muted glow, illuminating the astral surroundings and portraying a time when individuals, bound by the echoes of introspection, found solace in the shared stillness that enveloped them. Guided by the guardian's echo, the group navigated this astral realm with a shared acknowledgment of the delicate equilibrium. Symbols of revelation and interconnected destinies responded dynamically to their choices, weaving a narrative that connected the echoes of serenity with the challenges of the present. In the heart of the celestial nexus, the group confronted a manifestation of the astral currents—a convergence where the threads of fate intersected with the silent storm. Symbols of revelation and interconnected destinies pulsed with a tranquil yet foreboding energy, inviting the group to delve even deeper into the silent storm that lay ahead. With each reflection, the group embraced the echoes of serenity, recognizing the power that came from shared moments of stillness. The guardian's echo, a subtle melody in the cosmic currents, urged them to tread carefully through the silent storm, understanding that beneath the calm surface, profound changes and challenges awaited. As they moved through the celestial nexus, symbols of revelation and interconnected destinies continued to guide their path. The astral currents pulsed with the energy of anticipation, urging the group to explore further the silent storm and to discover the true extent of their collective resilience in the face of the unknown. In the aftermath of the celestial nexus, the group felt a sense of shared calm, aware that the silent storm held both challenges and opportunities. The guardian's echo, now a companion through the tapestry of serene memories, encouraged them to navigate the impending storm with unity and mindfulness, seeking to weave a new chapter in the interconnected destinies—one marked by shared stillness, anticipation, and the strength to face the echoes of desperation that still lingered.

The group, enveloped in the quiet anticipation of the silent storm, ventured deeper into the astral realms. The celestial anomalies unfolded like a darkened theater, with threads of fate weaving a mysterious narrative. The guardian's echo, now a whisper in the cosmic currents, guided them through the enigmatic landscape marked by the echoes of serenity and the impending storm. In this celestial anomaly, the group confronted echoes of mystery—a vision of the past where the threads of fate intertwined with moments of obscured truths and concealed revelations. Symbols of revelation flickered with an elusive glow, casting subtle shadows on the astral surroundings, portraying a time when individuals, bound by shared stillness, were on the precipice of unveiling the secrets that lay hidden. Guided by the guardian's echo, the group navigated this astral realm with a heightened sense of curiosity. Symbols of revelation and interconnected destinies responded dynamically to their choices, weaving a narrative that connected the echoes of mystery with the challenges of the present. In the heart of the celestial nexus, the group confronted a manifestation of the astral currents—a convergence where the threads of fate intersected with the enigmatic shadows. Symbols of revelation and interconnected destinies pulsed with an intriguing energy, inviting the group to delve even deeper into the mysteries that had long been shrouded in the silent storm. With each reflection, the group embraced the echoes of mystery, recognizing that the unveiling shadows held the potential to alter the course of their intertwined destinies. The guardian's echo, a cryptic melody in the cosmic currents, urged them to navigate the shadows with a blend of caution and courage, understanding that the truths they were about to uncover might reshape their journey. As they moved through the celestial nexus, symbols of revelation and interconnected destinies continued to guide their path. The astral currents pulsed with the energy of revelation, urging the group to explore further the unveiling shadows and to discover the true extent of their collective resilience in the face of hidden truths.

In the aftermath of the celestial nexus, the group felt a sense of trepidation mingled with curiosity, realizing that the silent storm was now on the verge of revealing long-concealed secrets. The guardian's echo, now a guide through the tapestry of mysterious memories, encouraged them to brace themselves for the revelations ahead, seeking to weave a new chapter in the interconnected destinies—one marked by discovery, understanding, and the strength to face the echoes of desperation that still lingered. As the group delved deeper into the astral realms, the silent storm intensified, and the cosmic currents began to resonate with an otherworldly tension. The celestial anomalies unfolded like ancient scrolls, unveiling secrets that had long been shrouded in mystery. The guardian's echo, now a haunting melody, guided them through the surreal landscape marked by the echoes of serenity and the impending revelation. In this celestial anomaly, the group confronted echoes of revelation—a vision of the past where the threads of fate intertwined with moments of profound discovery and the unfurling of hidden truths. Symbols of revelation radiated with an ethereal brilliance, illuminating the astral surroundings and portraying a time when individuals, bound by shared anticipation, stood on the precipice of unveiling the secrets that had remained obscured. Guided by the guardian's echo, the group navigated this astral realm with a mix of awe and trepidation. Symbols of revelation and interconnected destinies responded dynamically to their choices, weaving a narrative that connected the echoes of revelation with the challenges of the present. In the heart of the celestial nexus, the group confronted a manifestation of the astral currents—a convergence where the threads of fate intersected with the unrestrained revelations. Symbols of revelation and interconnected destinies pulsed with an intense, transformative energy, inviting the group to delve even deeper into the profound truths that awaited them in the silent storm. With each reflection, the group embraced the echoes of revelation, recognizing that the truths being unveiled had the power to reshape their understanding of the interconnected destinies. The guardian's echo, a haunting melody in the cosmic currents, urged them to approach the revelations with an open heart, understanding that the journey ahead held challenges and opportunities for growth.

As they moved through the celestial nexus, symbols of revelation and interconnected destinies continued to guide their path. The astral currents pulsed with the energy of transformation, urging the group to explore further the revelations unbound and to discover the true extent of their collective resilience in the face of profound truths. In the aftermath of the celestial nexus, the group stood on the precipice of newfound understanding, realizing that the revelations had begun to unbind the secrets that had long held sway over their destinies. The guardian's echo, now a guide through the tapestry of unveiled memories, encouraged them to embrace the transformative nature of the revelations, seeking to weave a new chapter in the interconnected destinies—one marked by acceptance, growth, and the strength to face the echoes of desperation that still lingered. The group, now standing on the precipice of profound revelations, pressed forward into the heart of the silent storm. The celestial anomalies unfolded with an intensity, each revelation a cosmic force shaping the threads of their interconnected destinies. The guardian's echo, a haunting refrain, accompanied them through a landscape transformed by the echoes of serenity and the revelations unbound. In this celestial anomaly, the group confronted echoes of transformation—a vision of the past where the threads of fate intertwined with moments of metamorphosis and the evolution of their shared understanding. Symbols of revelation shimmered with a kaleidoscopic brilliance, casting a surreal glow on the astral surroundings, portraying a time when individuals, touched by the revelations, began to undergo profound changes within. Guided by the guardian's echo, the group navigated this astral realm with a sense of awe and introspection. Symbols of revelation and interconnected destinies responded dynamically to their choices, weaving a narrative that connected the echoes of transformation with the challenges of the present. In the heart of the celestial nexus, the group confronted a manifestation of the astral currents—a convergence where the threads of fate intersected with the profound transformations. Symbols of revelation and interconnected destinies pulsed with an ethereal energy, inviting the group to delve even deeper into the metamorphic journey that awaited them. With each reflection, the group embraced the echoes of transformation, recognizing that the revelations had sparked an internal metamorphosis. The guardian's echo, a haunting refrain in the cosmic currents, urged them to navigate the transformative currents with courage and acceptance, understanding that the path ahead held both challenges and the promise of a renewed sense of unity.

As they moved through the celestial nexus, symbols of revelation and interconnected destinies continued to guide their path. The astral currents pulsed with the energy of rebirth, urging the group to explore further the echoes of transformation and to discover the true extent of their collective resilience in the face of profound change. In the aftermath of the celestial nexus, the group felt the echoes of transformation reverberating within, realizing that they had entered a new phase in their interconnected destinies. The guardian's echo, now a guide through the tapestry of metamorphic memories, encouraged them to embrace the changes, seeking to weave a new chapter in the interconnected destinies—one marked by resilience, acceptance, and the strength to face the echoes of desperation that still lingered. The group, now bathed in the afterglow of profound transformation, ventured further into the astral realms. The celestial anomalies unfolded with a newfound harmony, each revelation adding a layer to the evolving tapestry of their interconnected destinies. The guardian's echo, a serene melody, guided them through a landscape marked by the echoes of serenity and the transformative journey they had undertaken. In this celestial anomaly, the group confronted echoes of unity—a vision of the past where the threads of fate intertwined with moments of shared strength and the resilience that had emerged from the revelations. Symbols of revelation radiated with a serene luminescence, illuminating the astral surroundings and portraying a time when individuals, touched by the transformative currents, discovered a renewed sense of unity within themselves and with each other. Guided by the guardian's echo, the group navigated this astral realm with a shared commitment to resilient unity. Symbols of revelation and interconnected destinies responded dynamically to their choices, weaving a narrative that connected the echoes of unity with the challenges of the present. In the heart of the celestial nexus, the group confronted a manifestation of the astral currents—a convergence where the threads of fate intersected with the resilient unity. Symbols of revelation and interconnected destinies pulsed with a harmonious energy, inviting the group to delve even deeper into the bonds that had been fortified by the transformative journey.

With each reflection, the group embraced the echoes of unity, recognizing that their shared strength was an outcome of the challenges they had faced and the transformations they had undergone. The guardian's echo, a serene melody in the cosmic currents, urged them to cherish the resilient unity they had discovered and to face the challenges ahead with a unified front. As they moved through the celestial nexus, symbols of revelation and interconnected destinies continued to guide their path. The astral currents pulsed with the energy of solidarity, urging the group to explore further the echoes of unity and to discover the true extent of their collective resilience in the face of impending challenges. In the aftermath of the celestial nexus, the group stood united, fortified by the echoes of unity that resonated within. The guardian's echo, now a guide through the tapestry of harmonious memories, encouraged them to carry the spirit of resilient unity forward, seeking to weave a new chapter in the interconnected destinies—one marked by collective strength, understanding, and the unwavering determination to face the echoes of desperation that still lingered. Empowered by the echoes of unity, the group continued their journey through the astral realms, each step resonating with the newfound strength forged in the crucible of transformation. The celestial anomalies unfolded with a sense of continuity, each revelation interweaving seamlessly with the evolving tapestry of their interconnected destinies. The guardian's echo, a steady rhythm, guided them through a landscape marked by the echoes of serenity, resilience, and the ongoing odyssey of their shared existence. In this celestial anomaly, the group confronted echoes of continuity—a vision of the past where the threads of fate intertwined with moments of perpetual motion and the ongoing odyssey that defined their interconnected destinies. Symbols of revelation glimmered with a timeless radiance, illuminating the astral surroundings and portraying a time when individuals, sustained by the echoes of unity, embarked on a journey that transcended the boundaries of time and space. Guided by the guardian's echo, the group navigated this astral realm with a shared understanding of the ongoing odyssey they were undertaking. Symbols of revelation and interconnected destinies responded dynamically to their choices, weaving a narrative that connected the echoes of continuity with the challenges of the present.

In the heart of the celestial nexus, the group confronted a manifestation of the astral currents—a convergence where the threads of fate intersected with the eternal odyssey. Symbols of revelation and interconnected destinies pulsed with a timeless energy, inviting the group to delve even deeper into the essence of their shared journey that extended beyond the present moment. With each reflection, the group embraced the echoes of continuity, recognizing that their interconnected destinies were not confined by the boundaries of time. The guardian's echo, a rhythmic melody in the cosmic currents, urged them to cherish the ongoing odyssey and to face the challenges ahead with a sense of enduring purpose. As they moved through the celestial nexus, symbols of revelation and interconnected destinies continued to guide their path. The astral currents pulsed with the energy of perpetuity, urging the group to explore further the echoes of continuity and to discover the true extent of their collective resilience in the face of the ever-evolving journey. In the aftermath of the celestial nexus, the group felt a profound connection to the ongoing odyssey, realizing that their destinies were entwined in a tapestry that transcended the constraints of time. The guardian's echo, now a guide through the tapestry of perpetual memories, encouraged them to embrace the enduring nature of their interconnected destinies, seeking to weave a new chapter marked by continuity, purpose, and the unwavering commitment to face the echoes of desperation that still lingered. And so, with the echoes of continuity resonating in the cosmic currents, the group pressed on into the continuing cosmic tapestry, each step a testament to their enduring journey and the evolving nature of the interconnected destinies in the face of escalating desperation and the perpetual odyssey that bound them together.

Emboldened by the ongoing odyssey, the group moved deeper into the astral realms, where the celestial anomalies unfolded like pages of an ancient cosmic manuscript. The revelations of their interconnected destinies continued to shape the tapestry of their collective existence. The guardian's echo, now a harmonious cadence, guided them through a landscape marked by the echoes of serenity, resilience, and the ephemeral harmonies that resonated within the cosmic currents. In this celestial anomaly, the group confronted echoes of ephemerality—a vision of the past where the threads of fate intertwined with moments of fleeting beauty and the transient harmonies that graced their interconnected destinies. Symbols of revelation shimmered with a delicate luminosity, illuminating the astral surroundings and portraying a time when individuals, buoyed by the ongoing odyssey, reveled in the ephemeral harmonies that enriched their shared journey. Guided by the guardian's echo, the group navigated this astral realm with a profound appreciation for the transience of beauty. Symbols of revelation and interconnected destinies responded dynamically to their choices, weaving a narrative that connected the echoes of ephemerality with the challenges of the present. In the heart of the celestial nexus, the group confronted a manifestation of the astral currents—a convergence where the threads of fate intersected with the ethereal harmonies. Symbols of revelation and interconnected destinies pulsed with a gentle energy, inviting the group to delve even deeper into the essence of the transient beauty that adorned their ongoing odyssey.

With each reflection, the group embraced the echoes of ephemerality, recognizing that the beauty of their interconnected destinies was often found in the fleeting moments. The guardian's echo, a melodic serenade in the cosmic currents, urged them to savor the ephemeral harmonies and to face the challenges ahead with an awareness of the transient nature of their shared existence. As they moved through the celestial nexus, symbols of revelation and interconnected destinies continued to guide their path. The astral currents pulsed with the energy of fleeting beauty, urging the group to explore further the echoes of ephemerality and to discover the true extent of their collective resilience in the face of the ever-changing cosmic symphony. In the aftermath of the celestial nexus, the group felt a poignant connection to the ephemeral harmonies, understanding that their interconnected destinies were woven with delicate threads of transience. The guardian's echo, now a guide through the tapestry of fleeting memories, encouraged them to embrace the ephemeral beauty, seeking to weave a new chapter marked by appreciation, awareness, and the unwavering commitment to face the echoes of desperation that still lingered.

# Chapter 19: Final Gambit

The group, carrying with them the echoes of ephemerality, ventured further into the astral realms, where the celestial anomalies unfolded with an air of mystery. The revelations of their interconnected destinies had shaped a tapestry filled with fleeting beauty, but now they stood on the threshold of an unknown chapter. The guardian's echo, a soft whisper in the cosmic currents, guided them through a landscape marked by the echoes of serenity, resilience, and the veils of uncertainty that draped the cosmic expanse. In this celestial anomaly, the group confronted echoes of ambiguity—a vision of the past where the threads of fate intertwined with moments of obscured paths and the veils of uncertainty that shrouded their interconnected destinies. Symbols of revelation danced behind translucent screens, casting subtle shadows on the astral surroundings, portraying a time when individuals, touched by ephemeral harmonies, faced the enigmatic journey that lay ahead. Guided by the guardian's echo, the group navigated this astral realm with a blend of anticipation and caution. Symbols of revelation and interconnected destinies responded dynamically to their choices, weaving a narrative that connected the echoes of ambiguity with the challenges of the present. In the heart of the celestial nexus, the group confronted a manifestation of the astral currents—a convergence where the threads of fate intersected with the veils of uncertainty. Symbols of revelation and interconnected destinies pulsed with an elusive energy, inviting the group to delve deeper into the mysteries that veiled their ongoing odyssey. With each reflection, the group embraced the echoes of ambiguity, acknowledging that the journey ahead was draped in veils of uncertainty. The guardian's echo, a gentle murmur in the cosmic currents, urged them to step forward with courage and curiosity, understanding that the veils held both challenges and the promise of undiscovered revelations. As they moved through the celestial nexus, symbols of revelation and interconnected destinies continued to guide their path. The astral currents pulsed with the energy of the unknown, urging the group to explore further the veils of uncertainty and to discover the true extent of their collective resilience in the face of the enigmatic cosmic tapestry. In the aftermath of the celestial nexus, the group felt the weight of the veils of uncertainty, realizing that their ongoing odyssey was now intertwined with the mysteries that awaited. The guardian's echo, now a guide through the tapestry of obscured memories, encouraged them to embrace the unknown, seeking to weave a new chapter marked by courage, exploration, and the unwavering commitment to face the echoes of desperation that still lingered.

Guided by the guardian's echo, the group advanced into the depths of the astral realms, where the celestial anomalies seemed to thicken with an ethereal fog. The revelations of their interconnected destinies had led them to the veils of uncertainty, and now, they stood on the precipice of the unseen. The guardian's echo, a spectral murmur, gently led them through a landscape obscured by echoes of serenity, resilience, and the mysteries that lingered in the unseen realms. In this celestial anomaly, the group confronted echoes of the unseen—a vision of the past where the threads of fate intertwined with moments of hidden truths and the enigmatic echoes that reverberated through their interconnected destinies. Symbols of revelation flickered like distant stars, casting a faint glow on the astral surroundings, portraying a time when individuals, touched by the veils of uncertainty, ventured into the unseen with a sense of curiosity. Guided by the guardian's echo, the group navigated this astral realm with an air of anticipation. Symbols of revelation and interconnected destinies responded dynamically to their choices, weaving a narrative that connected the echoes of the unseen with the challenges of the present. In the heart of the celestial nexus, the group confronted a manifestation of the astral currents—a convergence where the threads of fate intersected with the echoes of the unseen. Symbols of revelation and interconnected destinies pulsed with a spectral energy, inviting the group to delve even deeper into the mysterious realms that unfolded beyond the veils of uncertainty. With each reflection, the group embraced the echoes of the unseen, acknowledging that the journey ahead was filled with hidden truths waiting to be discovered. The guardian's echo, a spectral melody in the cosmic currents, urged them to proceed with open minds and courageous hearts, understanding that the unseen held both challenges and the potential for profound revelations.

As they moved through the celestial nexus, symbols of revelation and interconnected destinies continued to guide their path. The astral currents pulsed with the energy of the undiscovered, urging the group to explore further the echoes of the unseen and to discover the true extent of their collective resilience in the face of the hidden mysteries. In the aftermath of the celestial nexus, the group felt the allure of the unseen realms, realizing that their ongoing odyssey was now entwined with the mysteries that lay just beyond the veils of uncertainty. The guardian's echo, now a guide through the tapestry of concealed memories, encouraged them to embrace the unknown, seeking to weave a new chapter marked by discovery, enlightenment, and the unwavering commitment to face the echoes of desperation that still lingered.

The group, now immersed in the veils of uncertainty and echoes of the unseen, pressed forward into the uncharted territories of the astral realms. The celestial anomalies seemed to respond to their presence with an eerie hush, as if the cosmic tapestry held its breath, awaiting the revelation of the hidden truths. The guardian's echo, a faint whisper, guided them through a landscape draped in mystery, resonating with the echoes of serenity, resilience, and the elusive whispers of the hidden. In this celestial anomaly, the group confronted echoes of the hidden—a vision of the past where the threads of fate intertwined with moments of cryptic knowledge and the concealed truths that defined their interconnected destinies. Symbols of revelation danced in the shadows, casting enigmatic patterns on the astral surroundings, portraying a time when individuals, drawn by the veils of uncertainty and the echoes of the unseen, sought to unravel the secrets that lay shrouded in the hidden realms. Guided by the guardian's echo, the group navigated this astral realm with a heightened sense of anticipation. Symbols of revelation and interconnected destinies responded dynamically to their choices, weaving a narrative that connected the echoes of the hidden with the challenges of the present. In the heart of the celestial nexus, the group confronted a manifestation of the astral currents—a convergence where the threads of fate intersected with the whispers of the hidden. Symbols of revelation and interconnected destinies pulsed with a clandestine energy, inviting the group to delve even deeper into the concealed truths that awaited them beyond the veils of uncertainty. With each reflection, the group embraced the echoes of the hidden, recognizing that the journey ahead was a quest for understanding the profound mysteries concealed within the cosmic tapestry. The guardian's echo, a subdued whisper in the cosmic currents, urged them to listen closely to the enigmatic whispers, understanding that the hidden held both challenges and the promise of profound revelations.

As they moved through the celestial nexus, symbols of revelation and interconnected destinies continued to guide their path. The astral currents pulsed with the energy of revelation, urging the group to explore further the echoes of the hidden and to discover the true extent of their collective resilience in the face of the cryptic knowledge that awaited them. In the aftermath of the celestial nexus, the group felt the weight of the hidden whispers, realizing that their ongoing odyssey was now intertwined with the enigmatic truths that lay concealed. The guardian's echo, now a guide through the tapestry of secretive memories, encouraged them to embrace the quest for the hidden, seeking to weave a new chapter marked by revelation, enlightenment, and the unwavering commitment to face the echoes of desperation that still lingered. And so, with the whispers of the hidden resonating in the cosmic currents, the group pressed on into the continuing cosmic tapestry, each step a testament to their readiness to uncover the concealed truths and the evolving nature of the interconnected destinies in the face of escalating desperation and the hidden whispers that beckoned them forward.

As the group delved deeper into the astral realms, the cosmic tapestry seemed to thicken with an air of anticipation, revealing cryptic signs that pointed to an intersection of destinies. The guardian's echo, now a subtle hum, guided them through a landscape marked by the veils of uncertainty, echoes of the unseen, and the mysterious whispers that permeated the hidden realms. In this celestial anomaly, the group confronted echoes of the cryptic—a vision of the past where the threads of fate intertwined with moments of intricate design and the enigmatic symbols that adorned their interconnected destinies. Symbols of revelation glowed with an arcane luminosity, casting complex patterns on the astral surroundings, portraying a time when individuals, drawn by the veils of uncertainty and the whispers of the hidden, arrived at a cryptic crossroads where choices held profound consequences. Guided by the guardian's echo, the group navigated this astral realm with a sense of solemnity. Symbols of revelation and interconnected destinies responded dynamically to their choices, weaving a narrative that connected the echoes of the cryptic with the challenges of the present. In the heart of the celestial nexus, the group confronted a manifestation of the astral currents—a convergence where the threads of fate intersected with the cryptic crossroads.

Symbols of revelation and interconnected destinies pulsed with an intricate energy, inviting the group to delve even deeper into the labyrinth of choices that awaited them within the hidden realms. With each reflection, the group embraced the echoes of the cryptic, understanding that the journey ahead was a delicate dance of deciphering the intricate symbols that adorned their interconnected destinies. The guardian's echo, a harmonious hum in the cosmic currents, urged them to approach the cryptic crossroads with wisdom and discernment, recognizing that each path held both challenges and the potential for transformative revelations. As they moved through the celestial nexus, symbols of revelation and interconnected destinies continued to guide their path. The astral currents pulsed with the energy of intricate design, urging the group to explore further the echoes of the cryptic and to discover the true extent of their collective resilience in the face of the profound choices that awaited them. In the aftermath of the celestial nexus, the group felt the weight of the cryptic crossroads, realizing that their ongoing odyssey was now intricately linked to the choices they would make within the hidden realms. The guardian's echo, now a guide through the tapestry of complex memories, encouraged them to navigate the cryptic with clarity, seeking to weave a new chapter marked by thoughtful choices, transformative revelations, and the unwavering commitment to face the echoes of desperation that still lingered.

As the group stood at the cryptic crossroads within the astral realms, the celestial anomalies unfolded with an intricate dance of cosmic energies, revealing pathways that led to unseen destinations. The guardian's echo, a melodic hum, guided them through the landscape marked by the veils of uncertainty, echoes of the unseen, and the enigmatic whispers that echoed through the hidden realms. In this celestial anomaly, the group confronted echoes of choices—a vision of the past where the threads of fate intertwined with moments of decision and the divergent paths that lay ahead in their interconnected destinies. Symbols of revelation flickered like lanterns along the astral pathways, portraying a time when individuals, enticed by the veils of uncertainty and the whispers of the hidden, stood at the labyrinthine crossroads where choices shaped the very fabric of their existence. Guided by the guardian's echo, the group navigated this astral labyrinth with a heightened awareness. Symbols of revelation and interconnected destinies responded dynamically to their choices, weaving a narrative that connected the echoes of choices with the challenges of the present. In the heart of the celestial nexus, the group confronted a manifestation of the astral currents—a convergence where the threads of fate intersected with the labyrinth of choices. Symbols of revelation and interconnected destinies pulsed with a dynamic energy, inviting the group to delve even deeper into the complex pathways that unfolded within the hidden realms. With each reflection, the group embraced the echoes of choices, recognizing that the journey ahead was a maze of possibilities. The guardian's echo, a guiding melody in the cosmic currents, urged them to navigate the labyrinth with intention and conviction, understanding that each decision held consequences that rippled through the interconnected destinies.

As they moved through the celestial nexus, symbols of revelation and interconnected destinies continued to guide their path. The astral currents pulsed with the energy of decisive moments, urging the group to explore further the echoes of choices and to discover the true extent of their collective resilience in the face of the intricate decisions that awaited them. In the aftermath of the celestial nexus, the group felt the weight of the labyrinth of choices, realizing that their ongoing odyssey was now intricately intertwined with the decisions they would make within the hidden realms. The guardian's echo, now a guide through the tapestry of decision points, encouraged them to choose wisely, seeking to weave a new chapter marked by thoughtful decisions, unforeseen revelations, and the unwavering commitment to face the echoes of desperation that still lingered.

# Chapter 20: Sunrise of Hope

The group, having traversed the labyrinth of choices within the astral realms, found themselves on the precipice of a cosmic convergence. The celestial anomalies resonated with the echoes of their journey—veils of uncertainty, whispers of the hidden, and the intricate choices that had shaped their interconnected destinies. The guardian's echo, a harmonious blend of all the melodies they had encountered, guided them through a final landscape marked by a sense of culmination and destiny. In this celestial anomaly, the group confronted echoes of convergence—a vision of the present where the threads of fate intertwined with moments of unity, understanding, and the culmination of their interconnected destinies. Symbols of revelation radiated with a resplendent glow, illuminating the astral surroundings and portraying a time when individuals, molded by their journey, stood at the nexus where destinies converged. Guided by the guardian's echo, the group moved through this astral realm with a shared sense of purpose. Symbols of revelation and interconnected destinies responded dynamically to their choices, weaving a narrative that connected the echoes of convergence with the challenges overcome and the resilience forged in the crucible of their shared odyssey. In the heart of the celestial nexus, the group confronted a manifestation of the astral currents—the ultimate convergence where the threads of fate interwove to form the grand tapestry of their destinies. Symbols of revelation and interconnected destinies pulsed with a transcendent energy, inviting the group to embrace the culmination of their interconnected journey.

With each reflection, the group embraced the echoes of convergence, realizing that their individual paths had led them to this moment of unity. The guardian's echo, a symphony of all the echoes they had encountered, urged them to appreciate the significance of their shared existence and to face the challenges that lay ahead with a collective strength forged through adversity. As they moved through the celestial nexus, symbols of revelation and interconnected destinies continued to guide their path. The astral currents pulsed with the energy of a shared destiny, urging the group to explore further the echoes of convergence and to discover the true extent of their collective resilience as they confronted the echoes of desperation one final time. In the aftermath of the celestial nexus, the group stood united, their destinies converged into a single harmonious melody. The guardian's echo, now a guide through the culmination of memories, encouraged them to carry the spirit of unity forward, seeking to weave a closing chapter marked by collective strength, understanding, and the unwavering commitment to face the echoes of desperation that lingered on the horizon.

# About the Author

I have been wanting to write books for a while but never knew how. When writing a book, I always go with something random and don't always know what I want to write about. Sometimes there are a lot of different reasons for this, but for me personally, I just think of something random and go with it. There are times when I will use an AI to help me, but I was just messing around. I love how this book turned out and I hope you enjoy it.

www.ingramcontent.com/pod-product-compliance
Lightning Source LLC
Chambersburg PA
CBHW071431130726
47997CB00006B/2042